BARE KNUCKLES JUSTICE

BY JOHN R. STANCZAK

Cover Illustration By: Susan Charest

There are those who seek knowledge for the sake of knowledge; that is curiosity. There are those who seek knowledge to be known by others; that is vanity. There are those who seek knowledge in order to serve; that is love.

St. Bernard

Then, say I…

There are those who seek knowledge by reading this book to attain enjoyment; that is genius.

ACKOWLEDGMENTS

Once again I am inclined to offer my deepest appreciation to my helpmates, Hannah, and Jordan Turner. In view of all of the unfortunate circumstances they have been faced with these past several months, I feel all the more indebted to them. Their professional touch with the editing process and the formatting procedure do much towards ensuring a polished final product. I truly mean it when I say that I could not have completed this journey without their expert help.

TABLE OF CONTENTS

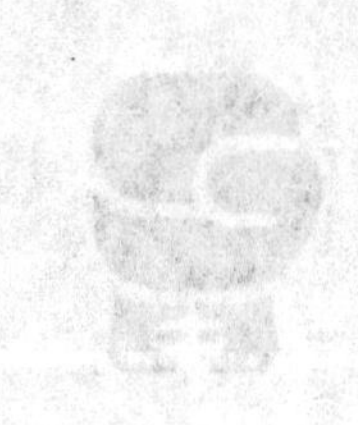

CHAPTER ONE:

THE NOT SO GOOD OLD DAYS

It seemed like only yesterday that Freddie Ryan was confronted by an older student on his way home from school. It was an unusually mild winter day in Paducah, Kentucky, his home for the last eight months of his young life. His dad's position, being a sales representative for a large pharmaceutical firm, required relocation in order to improve his job status. Each move was a step up the ladder and offered higher salaries. His trip home from school was not exactly his favorite time of the day, but as he trudged on toward home, he was in hopes of being greeted with a slice of fresh fruit pie. That was usually the case since he was the apple of his mother's eye. This welcome thought was interrupted when Freddie suddenly found himself face to face with none other than Bruno Balicki. Bruno the Bruiser, a nickname he acquired in his early age because he was prone to picking fights with anyone smaller than he was, demanded that Freddie hand over his lunch box. Much to Bruno's dismay, Freddie had eaten all that his mother had packed for his lunch that day. The empty lunch box infuriated Bruno, and he proceeded to exact some torture on his latest victim.

Upon arrival at home that night, Freddie was greeted by his loving mother, Maureen. She was visibly shaken by the appearance of her injured son. She questioned, "What happened to you?" Freddie answered, "You know old Balicki? Well, he beat me because he was upset that I didn't have any food in my lunch box." Mrs. Ryan responded, "Make sure you take steps to avoid him from now on. Did you fight back?" "No, you have always told me not to do so, and I didn't." She went on to tell him how proud she was of him for not getting involved in fights, and said he was a better person because of that. "Now go get cleaned up before your father comes home from work."

Dinner was served, and when the three of them had finished the meal, his mother went about cutting the piece of pie he longed for on the way home earlier in the day. It would be medicine to his bruised body. Freddie's father, Conor, had been eyeing him all through the meal and found it time to question him about his day. "Freddie, did something happen to you today?" Maureen was quick to cry out, "Dessert is served." Conor responded, "Good, we can talk about it while enjoying the pie." Maureen insisted that they enjoy their dessert so Freddie could get started on the large amount of homework he still had to complete.

After they had finished eating, Maureen quickly advised Freddie to go to his room and to start working on his assignments for the day. She started to busy herself with cleaning up the kitchen, and before Freddie could excuse himself, Conor said, "It looks as if we will have to have our discussion regarding my unanswered question tomorrow. Be prepared to do so as soon as I arrive home from work. Good night, son." A reply to his comment was quick in coming. "Yes sir, I'll be ready." Freddie moved on to his room while Maureen finished cleaning up the kitchen, and Conor sat down to read the newspaper before calling it a day. While in their bedroom preparing for sleep, Conor questioned Maureen about whether she knew anything about what might have happened. She replied, "I think you will have to pose that question to Freddie." Conor figured she was either being evasive or did not know any of the details. He gave her a goodnight kiss and wished her a restful sleep.

Freddie sat at the small table and finished the homework he had been assigned. His mind was fixated on the impending conversation with his father. *How do I please both my mother and my father?* He wanted so much to make that happen. It would be difficult to do because of the different outlook that his mom and dad had in regard to these types of encounters. Freddie's mom did not believe in an eye for an eye, while his father was of the mind that he should stand up and defend himself.

It was a fitful night of sleep for Freddie, and upon waking, his mind quickly focused on that evening. The school day that normally felt like it would never end went by awfully fast and it was not long before the bell sounded at the end of the school day. Unlike every other day, today there was no welcoming sound to it at all. He did take his mother's advice and selected a different route home, though, even the walk home seemed to be shorter than it normally was. Upon arriving home his mother advised him to complete his schoolwork before his father would get home. There wasn't even time for a piece of pie. Freddie thought these were all signs a bad outcome may result from their meeting.

The footsteps he would hear, that usually elicited excitement over the fact that his father had arrived, brought a sense of apprehension. Conor entered and bid hello to his wife and son and inquired about how everything went for them. He was almost half an hour later than usual and apologized for being tardy. He then suggested that they have dinner before having the discussion he had requested. Freddie wasn't sure whether he liked the idea or not. Maureen made the decision to eat first, figuring that small talk at dinner would be settling for Freddie and perhaps less time would be spent on the topic to be discussed.

It was an unusually quiet dinner that followed and one that seemed to put a strain on the usual delightful patter that was the norm. Freddie had lost his appetite many hours ago and halfheartedly poked at the food on his plate. To add to the somber air of the situation, there wasn't any pie for dessert. Upon completion of their meal, Conor suggested they get right down to the heart of the matter. Being the considerate and loving father that he was, and noticing Freddie's apparent concern about the impending discussion, he decided to soft-pedal the proceedings. That fact would be met with a great amount of approval from his mate.

"Freddie, could you briefly tell me exactly what happened to you yesterday?" Freddie related the incident concerning Balicki with hesitancy. He knew that what he had to say would not be pleasing to his father's ears. "Son, do you feel you did the right thing in the matter?" Again, Freddie reluctantly confessed that he had other thoughts on how he might possibly respond to Balicki's bullying. "I have always tried to respect yours and Mother's wishes, but that is hard to do when they conflict. In this matter, as well as on several other occasions, I chose to do as Mother had requested of me. It presents a definite problem to me when I am forced to decide as to whose wishes I should follow."

"I understand fully why it would trouble you, and I would like to explain to you and your mother why I feel that it is of considerable concern to me. I worry that by not defending yourself, you invite the aggressor to continue his assault on you. You also open yourself up to possibly sustaining a serious injury that may affect the quality of your life. If word gets around that you are an easy target who won't defend himself, it just may attract others to pounce on you. I don't want you to go looking for fights. Again, I only ask of you to defend yourself. You will probably find that these encounters will happen less frequently then, and possibly not at all. I also ask your mother to consider the advice that I have given you, and to make her decision known to you. I can only hope that it is one that we all agree upon, and we are in full accord that it is in the best interest of all of us."

Two weeks later Freddie would be put to the test while running an errand for his mother. As he walked along in search of the quilting kit that set him on this route, he encountered two young men who were students at the same high school he attended. He knew immediately that no good was to come of this chance meeting.

A taunting remark was directed to him as soon as they had met. One of the two prodded him, "Hey Freddie, I heard Balicki gave you a going-over the other day. Aren't you afraid to be out alone in danger of more of the same?" Freddie meekly responded, "I didn't come looking for trouble and don't expect any, nor have I done anything to merit it." The bigger of the two called out to his partner, "Hey, Ralph, did you just hear what I heard? He doesn't expect any. What do you think, Ralph? Is little Freddie in for some trouble he didn't expect? I don't know about you, but I think he is. In fact, I know he is."

Big Joe was through throwing remarks and started to throw punches that Freddie dodged by making some elusive moves. Freddie was in somewhat of a stupor due to the sudden confrontation and did not make any attempt to fight back. Ralph barked out, "He won't fight Joe, you need to give him reason to fight, if he is fool enough to attempt to try." Freddie backed off out of range of Joe's punches and insisted he did not want to fight since nothing was to be gained from doing so. Ralph blurted out, "Knock the hell out of that coward." Emboldened by his cohorts remarks Joe moved in to resume the fight. His thoughts were that it was going to be a very short one. Much to his surprise, he was met with three rapid punches from his intended victim. Now it was Joe who was looking at things much differently. He didn't like being on the end of taking some well-placed and effective punches. He yelled to his fellow belligerent, "Ralph, don't just stand there. Come and give me some help, you dummy." It happened that Ralph was not of much help due to two well placed punches on his proboscis that caused him to have a massive nosebleed. If Joe had intended to fight along with his partner in crime, it certainly did not appear to be the case. Two would-be tough guys were sent off on their way with their tails between their legs.

Freddie resumed his search for the quilting kits for his mother. He did not feel good about what had happened, and he hoped he would not be confronted with this situation again. As he continued on, Freddie reflected on the conversation with his father where the subject of protecting himself was broached. He realized the actions taken today were a result of his mother's advice to him. She said, "Freddie, I am not going to tell you what or what not to do when you get involved in a confrontation. You are a sensible and caring person capable of determining how to handle the situation. I am concerned either way when you are challenged to protect yourself. You can be hurt by turning your other cheek, as well as when you decide to stand up to defend yourself." He also gave some thought to his father's remark that by standing up to a threat it might result in a halt to the goading. He finally came across the store he was searching for and was able to purchase the item his mother wanted. She would certainly become the queen of the quilting group. He thought it was a pretty high honor considering she was a newcomer to "Quilt City," home of the National Quilt Museum.

Freddie remembered making three vows that day, one to his mother, another to his father, and finally one to himself. To honor his mother, he would always try to defuse a situation with common sense conversation. To his dad, by promising to defend himself should the need arise. And finally, to himself, that he would never tuck his tail between his legs when confronted. By adhering to them he would be able to please both parents and be true to himself.

Balicki heard about the fight Freddie had engaged in with Joe and Ralph, and decided he needed to test Freddie out again. That eventuality happened once again on what was a familiar path. The fight found both warriors suffering from some devastating blows, several of which drew blood. It would be said that there were no victors in the exchange, but it would be the last challenge ever directed at Freddie from Balicki.

However, it definitely was not the last fight that Freddie would have. It seemed there was always somebody wanting to garner the honor of whipping up on little Freddie Ryan, and Freddie was always ready to come to the aid of someone in need of a willing brawler.

That night at the Balicki household, Balicki was greeted with a harsh request wanting to know if he or his opponent came out better in the brawl. The senior Balicki blurted out, "From what I see it looks as though you may have been dealt the worst of it. Did you initiate the contact? If that is the fact, what do you intend to do about it? You know what I expect you to do. I want you to reengage with him and come out as the victor. A Balicki family member does not lose a fight he starts. Do things the Balicki way, the winning way, and do it soon. You don't want me to get involved do you?" Balicki pleaded with him, "No please, I will take care of the matter. I don't want to see someone be maimed." Mr. Balicki responded, "Time will tell. The matter is in your hands right now. Get it done." He slammed Bruno in the head with a few blows and told him, "If you don't there will be more of those coming."

CHAPTER TWO

DÉJÀ VU DISAPPOINTING RESULTS

It was the start of another day for Freddie Ryan, very much like most of the others he had experienced in recent months. He was in search of another job. Freddie, or Pug, as he was often called due to his pugilistic prowess, had a problem keeping a job. The fact that jobs were hard to come by, in addition to his tainted employment history, did nothing to aid him in his search. Employment was a sought-after prize at this time and employers could afford to be very fussy as to who they would take on as an employee. One thing was for sure in Freddie's case. He would not get a favorable recommendation from any of his previous employers. Inquiries about his job performance would inevitably elicit unfavorable responses that would be highly unlikely to lead to an offer. He was no stranger to the job search scene and was certainly not one to give up in his pursuit of a job of any kind.

As he disappointingly left the site of his latest interview, he started to think about the interviewer's last comment. The interviewer had informed him that it was not in the company's best interest to hire troublemakers, and this would most likely be the view of any company where he would seek employment. Freddie realized that his proclivity to engage in a fight anytime, anyplace, was not aiding him in his search.

Freddie left the interview feeling defeated. *I didn't start the fight; I was only trying to stop the scuffle before the old fellow was hurt.* Freddie never thought that trying to help quell a fight, especially an unevenly matched one, deserved a termination notice. What he considered to be the proper action at the time would haunt him as he searched for much needed employment. It just was not fair. However, Freddie was not of the mind to give up and vowed he would continue to search until he found something, anything. He couldn't be fussy.

Within a two week span he had engaged in seven interviews at different companies, each one with the same answer, "No, I am sorry we have nothing to offer." There were different reasons for not being able to offer employment, not qualified, overqualified, no previous experience, and mostly poor referrals from former employers. There was always some reason that hindered his chances. His lack of employment, and the continued inability to secure employment, soon became a point of contention with his father.

"Freddie, I am aware that the job market is not very kind to jobseekers at the present time, but surely there has to be an entry-level job of some sort out there in this big world. You have been job-hunting for over a month now. What are you being told by prospective employers?" "Well, Dad, to be very frank with you, it was the cause of my dismissal from my last employer that is the reason for my current situation. I was not honest with you when I told you that the company was downsizing. I was terminated because I interfered in an unfair fight between a strong thirty-year-old and a man who was in his late fifties. The older gent accidently dropped a casting on his aggressor's foot, who then went into a rage and started to pummel the old gent. I couldn't stand by and watch this play out, as I was concerned for the old man's well-being. My intent was to get between the two and stave off the attack. I soon became the target of the guy's onslaught and returned a couple of punches that put him down on the floor. It so happened that the bully had the onlookers testify to the fact that I had initiated the action, and that the old man threw the casting at his attacker. I am sure he had intimidated these fellows before and they were fearful of their well-being, leading to the false testimony."

Freddie was perplexed over the chain of events and unhappily provided, "I was tagged with the name Pug because I defended myself from a couple of guys shortly after the conversation we had some time back. Upon going to the defense of a helpless old fellow I now find myself unemployable. I do not favor the tag of Pug, and I don't like the position with which I am now faced. I don't have an answer as to what I need to do in order to solve the problem. Do you have any suggestions that might offer a solution?"

"Well, first of all, I am sorry to be hearing of this problem. You certainly don't deserve what has been handed to you. I, for one, do not see an immediate answer, and am under the opinion that you are going to be in a battle of a different sort trying to get out of this predicament. It is going to take dedication to the task, and you will have to persevere in your search. All I can offer is that you keep trying. If you fail to succeed you will have to try, try, try again. Be persistent in your search, and do not be afraid to promote yourself should the opportunity arise. Let them know of your accomplishments and explain what prompted your involvement in the various situations you might be questioned about. I will stand behind you in your efforts, and I will try to offer whatever assistance that I can. At present, all I am able to offer is my bid for you to be presented with good luck. I do want to be made aware of your progress or of any problems you might possibly incur. I am with you all the way."

Freddie persisted in his quest to find employment, but found no comfort being refused on five more attempts. Things were not looking good for him, and each successive trip to a potential employer became more painful. He knew the answer he would hear would not be to his liking. There had to be a job out there somewhere for him, and he would not give up until he found it.

Each evening as he came home from the job search, his father inquired whether he had found anything, and Freddie was becoming ashamed of the fact that his answer remained the same. He was concerned that he was not contributing anything to help satisfy the family's needs. After a brief period of silence, Conor, sensing Freddies feeling of inadequacy, offered words of encouragement to him and told him he felt something was going to work out very shortly.

The very next day during an interview at a small independent grocery store, the owner told Freddie that he would not let any of his past history influence his hiring decision. He went on to say that he was not hiring at the present time, and that he had two other applicants that would be vying for the next opening. "I am sorry about the trouble you have had finding work, but I assure you I will call you to let you know the decision I come to." Freddie left feeling that everything was going to end up with him working for a very fair boss.

Days turned into weeks and the job search continued with the same results. There was still no answer regarding the job at the grocery store. It was getting much more difficult to pursue the search especially when he received the same results at every interview. Freddie had resolved that if he was not the one awarded the position with the grocer, he would have to make some tough decisions that would be unpleasant for him, as well as for his parents.

On the way home that evening, Freddie thought about the possibilities open to him. He wished his grandfather was still alive, as he certainly would have welcomed Freddie and found work for him. He enjoyed the times he would go along with Gramps and watch him trim and shoe horse's hooves. Freddie loved living in The Plains, a small rural town located in Fauquier County in Virginia. It was in the heart of horse country and the home of The Virginia Gold Cup Race, which had been held in Fauquier County since 1922. Freddie thought about the excitement during race season when the field of horses showcased their athleticism hurdling the many barriers on the racecourse. The sound of the pounding hooves and the grunts coming from the horses and jockeys was like a symphony to his ears. He envisioned being there as he continued making his way back home. He noted that the damp weather in Paducah, with the Ohio River running through the town, was so much different than the dry humid air he had come to enjoy in The Plains. *The move could be possible even though Gramps was no longer living.*

Within a few minutes his mind began to focus on another alternative that was particularly pleasing to him. He thought about joining the Army, an idea that crossed his mind on many occasions. It was his opinion that he was suited for service life, but Freddie knew very well that his mother would object to his notion of joining the Army. After much thought given to the matter, he figured he would put both choices on a side burner for the time being. He was tired and wanted to be home.

Two weeks later he was surprised by a telephone call from the friendly grocer. Upon hearing who the caller was, he immediately felt he would soon be working for him. However, this was not to be the case, and the owner apologized that he would not be the new hire. He did say that he would keep Freddie in mind for the very next opening that became available.

CHAPTER THREE:

PERSEVERANCE GETS RESULTS

It was in early spring that Freddie "Pug" Ryan became a believer that miracles do happen. He received an early morning call from a prospective employer informing him that she would like to speak to him regarding an employment opportunity. The excitement was building as he dressed for the occasion. There could not have been a more excited and hopeful young lad in Paducah that day. The first order of business was to let his mother and father know what he had just learned.

"Mom and Dad, you are not going to believe it, but I just got word that I have been made a job offer. I can hardly believe it myself. Me, Freddie Ryan is soon to be 'hard working Freddie Ryan.'" His mother was the first to speak, saying, "Freddie I am so proud of you, and I hope that your employer realizes what a fine young man he will have working for him." His father was quick to add, "I am equally proud of your achievement, and just as I recently told you, I knew something would be offered to you soon. I give you credit for persisting in spite of the many refusals, and I must say you never showed signs of being indolent in your search."

Freddie was walking on air as he left the house that morning a new man. There was nothing that would hold him down. A delightful sense of worth permeated his whole being as he briskly ventured on to meet his soon-to-be employer. The air felt fresher, the sun was shining brighter, and the people he passed were all happier than usual. This was indeed a glorious day for Freddie. He wondered if his new boss would have the same feelings that he had.

As he entered the store, a feeling of apprehension invaded his state of euphoria. His thoughts shifted. *Can I do the job? Am I smart enough to learn? Will she like me? Am I lacking anything I need to perform? Will I get along with the other workers and not have problems?* He looked around and liked what he saw and felt like this was going to be a good place to work and learn. *Who knows, someday, I could be the boss here.*

Within a few minutes, a smartly dressed and attractive young lady approached him and introduced herself. She posed the question, "Are you here regarding the job opening?" She was greeted with Freddie's answer, "Yes ma'am, I am." She promptly replied, "I am Gloria Brooks. Would you follow me to the office please?" Gloria was all business and wasted no time launching into some preliminaries prior to the orientation process. Upon delivering a cordial greeting, she informed Freddie that his persistence was the reason he was sitting there today. She also acknowledged that the demeanor and attitude he presented when being informed at his three previous interviews with her that a position was unavailable was admirable and well noted. Her last comment was, "I feel that I should inform you that the behavior you displayed at your last place of employment has no place here and will not be tolerated under any circumstance."

"With that being said, and totally understood by you, let's get down to the business of acquainting you with our company's rules, regulations, and lastly the benefits you will be offered."

She went on explaining all of the necessary information and was quite pleased by his attentiveness to the proceedings. "I want you to know that this can be a difficult job at times. You will be asked on many occasions to do things that you may find beneath you, but they must be completed. It is of utmost importance that our customer be given willing aid and that it is delivered in a courteous manner." Her immediate thoughts were that she was dealing with someone who was highly likely to become a star employee. "Well, Mr. Freddie Ryan, I want to be the first to greet you as our newest employee. It is my feeling that you will become a valuable team member who will be with us for a long time. I will introduce you to the rest of the associates, show you around to the various departments, and issue you the required uniform you will need while at work. After lunch, you will meet the Store Manager, and our owner, Mr. Swanson."

They broke for lunch, and while eating in the associate's break room, Freddie had the opportunity to meet Ty Foster, Produce Manager, and one of his employees, Enzo Barone. He enjoyed their company as well as the conversation that took place, but it was soon time to return to Ms. Brooks and get on with the rest of the day. "Are you ready to meet the owner, Mr. Swanson? He is awaiting our arrival, so we had better get a move on. I think you will like him. He is very unpretentious and easy to converse with. He may make you a bit uneasy because of his intense focus on you as you answer his questions. Ms. Brooks knocked lightly on his open office door, leaned in, and inquired if he was ready for them. He blurted out, "I am always ready for Freddie," and chuckled at his comment. He thought it was pretty witty. It was a short, informal meeting, lacking the many anticipated questions Freddie expected to be asked of him. Freddie found Mr.

Swanson to be quite cordial and very perceptive. He definitely noticed his piercing gaze while listening to the answers to the few questions he asked.

After leaving the office, Ms. Brooks told Freddie, "Your visit was much shorter than most introductory meetings. Mr. Swanson was apparently at ease with you and had no need for a barrage of questions. I felt that you presented yourself well, which explains the lack of questions being posed." Freddie felt good about the meeting and was impressed with the professional manner of Mr. Swanson.

The first day at Swanson's Supermarket went famously and on his way to the house he was revisited by all the good feelings he had on the way to his first day of work. He could not believe that he was actually fully employed and found it even harder to believe he would be receiving pay for the day. He reflected on the past couple of months and was happy they were behind him. He was well pleased with the Store Manager, fellow co-workers, and felt he had also made a new friend in Enzo from the Produce Department. He wondered if it could get any better.

CHAPTER FOUR:

CELEBRATION TIME

When Freddie opened the door to enter the house, he was greeted by a host of friends and some out-of-town relatives who had been invited to celebrate his success. Seeing his uncle, aunt, and two cousins, who were his favorite relatives, was quite a surprise. It was fortunate that they were passing through on their way to Keeneland in Lexington, Kentucky. It was a festive occasion, with a wonderful meal offering all of his favorite choices, including the best apple pie his mother had ever baked. The gathering lasted into the early evening hours and allowed for some cherished visiting time with his two cousins. Conor politely suggested that the evening would have to come to a close in order for the newly hired hand to get a good night's sleep and not be late for work in the morning. Long hugs and goodbyes were in order, and soon the three of them found themselves alone savoring their good fortune.

The second day of work at Swanson's saw him leaping out of bed to prepare for another great day. His mind raced a mile a minute as he hurriedly walked on. Freddie did not want to be late for work. There was nothing he would consciously do to spoil the tremendous, good fortune he had received. All went well on his second day and likewise for the rest of the week. Ms. Brooks was very attentive to his every need and made sure that he was being properly trained. It was necessary that he be advised as to how to properly interface with the various departments in order to assure excellent customer service. As he was moved from department to department, something in the pharmacy caught his eye and left him somewhat bewildered. That Friday, Freddie found himself in the storage area, rounding out his visits to all of the departments in the store. The Grocery Department, as this area was referred to, was of the most interest to him. It appeared to him that working in this department offered the greatest opportunity for advancement. He also liked the fact that it would offer him the chance to be most available to the customer. He liked to be of service to people. While in this department, Freddie became curious about the number of what appeared to be non-employees lingering near the docks at the rear of the store.

A tired, and highly inspired Freddie was very happy about all he learned in a few short days. Ms. Brooks intercepted him as he headed to the employee lounge to clock-out and call it a day. "Well, Freddie, how do you feel this week went for you? Was there any department that caught your interest? Do you have any questions for me?" "Everything went great for me, Ms. Brooks. I really feel like I learned a lot. As far as the department that is of most interest to me, I would say the Grocery Department." "And why was that, Freddie?" "Well, Ms. Brooks, one has the freedom of being in all parts of the store, which offers the most opportunity to be of immediate service to the customer." "I find your comment to be very interesting and well received. There is an opening in the department, and it happens to be a daytime slot. Would you like to talk to the department manager? He has final say about the selection of the person seeking work in his department. If you would like I will set up an appointment with him for 8:00 a.m., Monday morning." Freddie excitedly replied, "I would love that." She told him, "It's a done deal. Don't be late. He is a stickler about punctuality."

Freddie was happy and satisfied and couldn't help but think, *I have found employment, and more notably it could be in the department of my choice. That is if Mr. Gaines finds me acceptable.* The trip home is full of other thoughts that lingered on in his mind. He also thought about the following week when he would bring home his first paycheck. The next thought was that he would buy a nice prime rib roast for Sunday's dinner and a nice bouquet of flowers for his mother. He figured that his dad's gift would be eating his share of the fine roast superbly cooked by his loving wife.

A new week had dawned, and Freddie was excitedly preparing for work. It was the day he was to meet with Fred Gaines, who hopefully would become his boss. He was told to stop in at Ms. Brooks' office prior to his meeting with him. He arrived much before his regular start time and sat outside of her office waiting for her arrival. He didn't have to wait long as she arrived a few scant minutes after he did. He barely had time to sit down before she came. "Good morning, Freddie. My, you are here bright and early. You will have to wait a few minutes as I have some business to attend to before I can meet with you. It should not take long for me to complete what I have to do." While Freddie waited, he could hear that she was engaged in a conversation. She had to have been on the phone as the only voice he heard was hers. When she returned to invite him into her office, he noticed a remarkable change in her. She seemed to be very upset and concerned, possibly as a result of the conversation she had just finished. "Freddie, come on in and sit for a minute. I wanted to wish you success with your meeting this morning. I feel confident that you will be met with Mr. Gaines' approval. If that should not be the case, come back to my office, and we will figure out where to go from there. If you do meet with his approval, I would like to see you after your training ends for the day. I would like your feedback as to how your meeting went."

He clocked in for the day and immediately proceeded to the small office of the grocery manager. The door was open, and he could see that Mr. Gaines was busy at his desk. He approached his office and was about to knock on the open door. Fred Gaines had seen him approaching and hurriedly put the tablet that was the focus of his attention into the top desk drawer. "Come on in, son. Have a seat and get comfortable. I have some hot coffee left in the pot. Would you care to have a cup?" "No thank you, sir, I am not a coffee drinker." Gaines chuckled and replied, "I am glad to hear that. Some of these guys spend a bit too much time drinking coffee. I usually ask the question of applicants as to why they want to work in this department. I don't need to do so with you because Brooks has already informed me of your reason. She seems to be quite preferential in her dealings with you. Is there a family relationship?" "No, not at all. I really do not want special treatment. I just want to do my job the best that I can." Gaines continued and asked, "You seem to want to have contact with the customer. That surprises me. I would have thought that with your past history you would want to shy away from contact. Am I wrong in thinking that way?" "I'm not quite sure what you are referencing." "Freddie, surely you have recollection of some of the fights you have been involved in, which caused you problems securing employment? The fact is that some of them have taken place at one or another of your workplaces. Is that not true?" Freddie confirmed, "There was a recent incident that happened while at work. I attempted to break up a fight between a pair where there was a vast age difference between them. I was concerned about the older man's well-being. The fact is the younger fellow was the aggressor in the matter." "If that was the case, why were you dismissed and not him?" "It seems the man was able to convince fellow employees to testify to the fact that I initiated the action." "Are you telling me that you were wrongly accused in the matter?" "I absolutely was, and I stated the fact to the Human Resources Officer that heard the case." "He apparently did not believe you?" "No, he did not." "Okay, then I would like to change the subject a bit here and ask how you feel about certain things. Do you take drugs?" "No, I do not." "Do you feel it wrong for someone to take drugs?" "If we are talking about illegal drugs, then I would say it is absolutely wrong. Poisoning your body is certainly not in one's best interest." "What do you think should be done to people who sell illegal drugs?" "They should be effectively dealt with by the law enforcement agencies." "Freddie, you certainly have the answers, but I am not sure that I believe all of them. I don't believe that you are a good fit for the vacancy that I am trying to fill, and I will have to keep looking for the right person for the position. Thank you for giving consideration towards doing so. I wish you luck in your next selection of choice. I am sure that Ms. Brooks will have the right place for you."

As Freddie exited the office after the interview, he was gravely concerned about his future with the Swanson Supermarket. He was a very dejected fellow, much different from the one he was that morning when he left home for work. While walking out of the grocery area, he once again noticed a group of young men, who he was sure were not company employees, gathered together.

He hastened on to the office of Gloria Brooks to inform her that he had struck out with Mr. Gaines. She was there waiting for him and was not happy upon hearing his news. "How do you think your interview went today? Were you bothered by anything that transpired?" Freddie was quick to say, "It felt more like an inquisition than an interview. I do not understand all of the questions about drugs that were thrown at me. I am not a drug addict. I was of the opinion that those are questions to be dealt with prior to being hired." "You are right about that. I will deal with Mr. Gaines to assure you we have no repeat performances. Sorry that I put you through that. Now let's go to the department that I originally hired you for. All right then? You can come with me."

It was a totally different experience he had with the customer service manager, Ed Frye, who greeted him and immediately recognized him as his new employee. Ms. Brooks did not linger much after the initial exchange between Freddie and Mr. Frye and bid both of them a good day. She ended her stay by wishing Freddie good luck in his new position. The events of the time spent in what would be his assigned department revitalized him, and the ever-present smile was back on his handsome young face. The rest of the day was spent with Mr. Frye showing him around the department, introducing him to fellow employees and familiarizing him with the equipment and procedures. There was a lot to be learned, and he was eager to get on with doing so. It seemed

that the end of the day was upon him much before he was
ready to quit learning. He knew this is where he belonged.

The next day found an eager and enthusiastic young man
happily on his way to work. Freddie arrived and was warmly
greeted by Ed Frye. When he returned the good morning
salutation, addressing him as "Mr. Frye," he was asked to
address him as Ed in the future. "We are fellow employees,
and I see no reason for formalities when addressing each
other. I for one appreciate a relaxed and courteous
atmosphere in the department. My thought is that by doing
so we all become more productive in our work. Speaking of
work, let's you and I get about the business of continuing our
training sessions." The rest of the time was spent doing
exactly that and was done in a very professional and pleasing
manner. Again, a tired and enthusiastic trainee had come to
the end of a day he found much satisfaction with.

The next two days were spent learning just about all that
could be explained to him. The rest of his learning would be
accomplished in an on-the-job mode. He was able to spend
some time getting better acquainted with fellow employees
while Ed tended to some of his managerial duties. It was time
well received by him as he wanted to get more familiar with
the people he would be working with. He had the pleasure of
being introduced to another bright and pleasant young man,
Toby, who had been placed on the job a short six months
ago. He next met Ling-Su, who was in the department in a
manager-trainee position. She had been transitioning from
one department to another in order to learn all she could
about each person and their responsibilities. The last person
met that day was a healthy-looking individual who presented
a picture of being blessed with both brains and brawn. His

immediate thought was that he did not belong there. He envisioned Bruce Cannon as perhaps a health instructor, possibly an athletic coach, or maybe even a star athlete. He was a person that not only intrigued Freddie, but one he felt most comfortable with and trusting of.

Ed soon returned to request Freddie's attention and spent the rest of the day informing him of what he was expected to accomplish on his final training day. Another productive learning day had been completed, leaving both the trainer and the trainee very pleased with the results. "Freddie, I will see you bright and early tomorrow. Be prepared for a whirlwind of a day. I advise a good night's sleep to help you cope with your upcoming tests." "Alright, be assured that I will be here early, prepared for the tests, but most likely not rested. I will probably have a problem falling asleep tonight."

Friday, the last day of work, test day, and happily his first payday, had arrived. True to his word he was at work early and appeared to be very well rested. Ed greeted him with a smile, and questioned him, "Are you ready for the buzzsaw?" "They don't call me "Ready Freddie" for nothing. Bring it on." The day proved to be a wild success for Freddie. He aced all of the tests and was graded very highly by the associates that he was placed with during the on-the-job-training process. Ed Frye was very pleased with the results and seemed to be on cloud nine along with his trainee. The department had prepared a surprise celebration, and they all took time to enjoy a piece of freshly baked spice cake from the bakery. Ed awarded him with his first paycheck that Gloria Brooks made sure was in the proper department for distribution. The day turned out to be very eventful for all the members of the Customer Service Department.

On his way home, Freddie had two stops to make, one to
Kellys' Butcher Shop for a nice prime rib roast, the other to
Katy's Floral Garden for an aromatic bouquet of flowers. It
was nice and convenient for him since they were across the
street from one another. The time spent walking home
allowed for time to consider all that had happened in the span
of one week. He realized that he'd had feelings of sheer
happiness to utter disillusionment, and back again to
somewhat thrilled. There was so much on his mind that he
did not know how to filter everything out. He almost forgot
that he needed to stop at the bank to make his first deposit
into his savings account. The amount deposited would leave
sufficient funds for his intended purchases, a sum to present
to his parents, as well as enough to cover snacks for him for
the week. He made the appointed stops and was bursting
with anxiety and a need to get home to make his presentation.
He wanted so much to please his loving mother.

Upon his arrival home, Fred was greeted by his mother and
promptly presented her with the lovely bouquet of flowers.
His gesture brought tears of sheer joy to her eyes and caused
her to choke up while thanking him profusely. She asked,
"What do you have in the bag?" "Our dinner for tonight. I
originally wanted it for Sunday's dinner. It's time to celebrate,
don't you agree?" "I celebrate you every day for being the
good son that you are. I consider myself to be very lucky to
have you. Tell me, how did the day go for you?" "Well let me
say the whole week has been like being on a teeter-totter. It's
like I am up then down and ending it somewhere in between.
I have so many questions that need answers, and I am
wondering if the bubble is about to burst. I am a bit

concerned about what the future may bring." "Why are you feeling that way?" "One reason is due to a troubling interview I had with a manager of a department in which I had wanted to be placed. The second is because of several happenings I observed that seem to be irregular and out of place. There also seems to be some strange behavior on the part of some of the managerial staff, some mistrust among them. It puzzles me greatly."

It was not long before Conor made his entrance just as the conversation had taken an abrupt ending. It left Freddie heading to his room to wash the grocery business off of him. It did nothing to get any of it off of his mind. Maureen was bewildered. She did not know what to make of the situation. Conor gave her a hearty hello, along with a peck on the cheek and questioned, "What are we having for dinner?" "Tonight, we are celebrating our son's first week at his new job, and he brought home a beautiful bouquet of flowers for me." "That's not what we are having for dinner, is it?" "No smarty, he also brought home a perfect prime rib roast. I would have thought you'd recognize that wonderful aroma?" "I guess I blew it again." She retorts, "Just slightly."

Conor and Freddie were seated as Maureen placed the last serving dish on the table to complete the offerings for the evening's meal. Conor proceeded to offer grace for the wonderful feast they were about to enjoy and called for blessings for the fantastic cook. He also took the opportunity to offer an invocation seeking continued success for Freddie's future. "It's celebration time, let's eat and enjoy this wonderful evening." All this time, Freddie was in a pensive mood and wondered if this celebration was warranted. He

was not feeling too sure of what the future had in store for
him.

CHAPTER FIVE:

LEARNING THE ROPES

The next couple of weeks did not present an incident of any
sort that would cause concern for Freddie. He was highly
engrossed in learning all he could about the job and found
much pleasure while doing so. His devotion to his work did
not go unnoticed by his admiring manager, who felt that he
was a model employee. His attention to detail along with his
desire to please the customer was apparent to all of the
department associates. Freddie's work ethic was quickly
recognized by the mysterious Bruce Cannon and garnered
some glowing remarks from him. As time passed a bond
formed between the two of them. There was a mutual respect
that seemed to be shared by the pair.

Whatever time was left after finishing his lunch was used to
wander through the store to get acquainted with other
departments' associates. His thought was that some of those
he met were open to his quest to become familiar, while
others preferred to remain standoffish. He didn't give much
thought as to why that was the case other than the fact that
some people were slow to warm up to new acquaintances. He
may have given the same impression sometimes while
meeting new people and shrugged off the incident. On his
return to his department, he noticed two associates' attention
being diverted toward him, causing some uneasiness. He

could not be positive but felt like one of the two might have been Toby. His uncertainty of the fact was due to his line of sight being obstructed by shoppers in the aisle.

Back at work and near quitting time, for no apparent reason to him, Freddie was suddenly overcome with a TGIF feeling. It may have been due to the fact that it was Friday and also payday. It might also have been because he had made arrangements to get together with Enzo Barone on Saturday. Again, this week was another that did not foster a reason for a family celebration. No need existed for purchases of prime rib or flowers today. On the way home he would stop at the bank and make his weekly savings deposit, keeping some cash to help with family expenses and enough for his lunch and snack needs. *I am really a fortunate guy.*

The walk home was refreshing, a light breeze was blowing slightly warm air that provided a buffer against a sunless cloudy day. He was hoping that there was no rain in tomorrow's forecast. He wanted a nice day for his outing with Enzo. Neither of them had a car and would be walking a lot when not on the bus. For whatever reason, he was hungrier than usual and was anxious to get home in order to kick back and rest up for tomorrow's escapade.

He arrived home, greeted his mother, and proceeded to tell her about the day's activities. There was not a whole lot to talk about, which was pleasing to Maureen's ears. She was glad that it was another day without any problems. She was thinking that all would be well from here on out. Conor was a little late in getting home and Freddie was anxious for his arrival to happen soon. He was super hungry. He didn't have to wait too much longer for his dad's arrival and was really happy when he came through the door. Conor must have been just as hungry as his son, and questioned, "Is dinner about to be served?" Maureen promptly replied, "It will be on the table and waiting for you as soon as you get freshened up." And so, it was. Hot and tantalizing food was at their disposal, and soon was being enjoyed by the Ryan family. There was no time for small talk and the banter was kept to a minimum. What little there was had the sole purpose of praising the cook for the wonders of the meal. It ended on a happy note as the dessert today was a delicious cherry pie, a change of pace that was well received by the male members.

The table was cleared of the dishes, and Maureen topped off the coffee cups and sat down to listen to news Conor had been made aware of today. It was news delivered after working hours and accounted for his delay in arriving home late. The Paducah Police Department had detailed an officer to come to Conor's office to alert all drug salespeople of an uptick in drug activity in the area. He had been informed that the areas between Clarksville, Tennessee, including Fort Campbell, Hopkinsville, Murray, and Paducah in Kentucky, along with Marion, and Carbondale in Illinois, showed signs of large increases in new cases. It appeared to law enforcement that there seemed to be some involvement of individuals from drug companies. A teenage boy was near death from an overdose but was saved by the fast thinking and instant treatment by a law enforcement officer who responded to a frantic plea from the boy's mother. They asked for full cooperation in the matter and immediate information about any drug activity that office staff become aware of. The officer said that the drug dealers were concentrating their efforts at colleges and universities, high schools, and the more affluent residential areas. Maureen asked, "Are you concerned about the police stating somebody in the sales of pharmaceuticals is entangled in the problem?" "I don't feel that I should be concerned personally, but I do not like the idea that there might be somebody involved." Maureen replied, "I am sure that you will not see the last of that man. I feel positive that you are a suspect at this time and are being watched." With that being said, a hush fell about them, and the conversation came to a sudden halt. Freddie's mind turned to the empty pill bottles he observed while touring the departments at the time of his orientation. *I think it is time for another visit to the pharmacy.*

The three of them retired to the living room to catch the evening news before calling it a day. There was no news regarding any drug activity, not even a mention of the young lad that was supposed to have been near death. As soon as the news hour had ended, they all had the same idea about getting on to bed for some restful sleep.

Waking up to the bright sunshine and what looked to be the start of a beautiful day was very pleasing to Freddie. He was looking forward to what the day would bring for him and his new acquaintance, Enzo. He remembered being told by him to wear sweats or clothing that could take a bit of punishment. He didn't own any sweats, so he put on a well-worn flannel shirt and an old pair of jeans. He joined his parents for the usual big breakfast they would enjoy on Saturday mornings. It was, as usual, a very appetizing meal for which he gratefully thanked his mother and father, then bid them farewell for the day. He was sure he would be home much before dinner time and told them of his plans for the day. They bid him a good day and advised him to be careful. Mom added, "You can expect an apple pie for dessert, so don't fill up on junk food." "I assure you I won't let that happen."

He moved along at a fast pace anxious to get to the agreed upon meeting place to join his newfound friend. When he arrived, he was greeted by Enzo. "So, Enzo, where to first?" "There is a place I go to every Saturday morning that I'd like to show you. I am sure you will like it." "I'm sure that I will, so let's get on the move. I'm eager to see it."

It was a good distance to their destination, a gym he frequented every Saturday morning. The owner, retired Army Seargent Brixton Jay Whitney had remodeled an old hay barn which was left to him by his late father. Brixton, or B.J. as he was referred to by everyone familiar with him, had no intentions of farming and decided to do what he knew best. As a member of the cadre for his assigned basic training unit, B.J. conducted the physical training for the recruits. Additionally, he was the coach of the Fort Riley boxing team at Fort Riley, Kansas. His goal was to have the best gym in Paducah, Kentucky where he would train aspiring young men in the art of boxing. Fortunately for him, the city sprawl reached out into the country. County road AA separated his property from the city proper. Where the deer used to roam were large developments, with houses springing up at a rapid rate. After adding two wings to the existing structure, he was able to accommodate all of the equipment he would need to ply his trade. A good honest man had successfully opened up his dream business to the delight of quite a few fitness seekers.

A good bit of light conversation was exchanged on the way to the gym between what seemed to be two longtime friends. They arrived at what was an older neighborhood and stopped in front of a wooden structure that resembled an old saloon one might have seen in an old western movie. It appeared to be well maintained for its age, and hanging from above the wide front entrance was a large sign. The message, "WE TURN BOYS INTO MEN," in bold red letters printed on it was sure to attract one's attention. In smaller black letters on another sign was printed, "ASK ARNOLD HE CAN VOUCH FOR THAT." Below that sign hung a much smaller one identifying the owner, B.J. WHITNEY Esq. Freddie was flabbergasted, and did not speak for what seemed to be an eternity. "Is something wrong?" "Oh, no, nothing like that. I guess I'm just a bit surprised by it. Let's go in, I want to see the inside."

Once inside, they were greeted by a boisterous B.J. who heartily welcomed both of them. "Enzo, how are you doing, and who is your fine feathered friend you have dragged in here? Freddie laughed, and Enzo jokingly said, "The next welterweight boxing champion of the world." Nothing further was said by Freddie, who was now gazing at one of the rare modern pieces of equipment in the gym. A very well-kept boxing ring took center stage in the building, while all around it were other fine pieces of equipment. One of the Everlast personal boxing bags was being punished by a sizeable young man. Two of the many speed bags that were located throughout the gym were being rattled at a rapid pace by what appeared to be well trained wannabes. The sound of heavy metal meeting the concrete floor rattled as weightlifters dropped the barbells upon completing their weightlifting sessions. The place was abuzz with frenetic activity throughout the entire building. B.J. inquired, "Enzo, are you and the future champ going to go a few rounds?" Freddie was quick to respond, "I am much safer as an observer. I might like to try to see how I do on a speed bag. I also want to watch Enzo in action." He looked at him and asked, "Am I going to get the chance to see that?"

Freddie got some bag gloves from B.J. and began to clumsily punch at the speed bag, while Enzo did some preliminary warm-up routines prior to getting in the ring with a selected partner. B.J. had his eyes on Freddie, who was observing others who were going through some speed bag routines. He never had punched one before and felt quite inadequate about his performance. He was a good observer and a quick learner. In a short time, Freddie was rattling the bag at a fairly fast pace. There was no doubt that he had very good hand eye coordination. It was evident that his rhythm would allow for him to land a damaging counterpunch on an opponent coming in on him. B.J. was surprisingly impressed at what he was observing and did nothing to interrupt Freddie's session. He wanted to see what his capabilities were without him being aware that he was being closely scrutinized. Freddie kept punching for some time and his rhythm and speed steadily increased. He finally had enough and wanted to be at ringside when Enzo started his sparring session.

Enzo had just climbed up and was parting the ropes in order to get into the ring. Once in, he started to shuffle around in his corner and took up a bladed stance, quickly moving into a forward shuffle. He moved to a lateral shuffle, made a pivot, a couple of L steps and another quick pivot, then another pivot, before feigning a counter punch. Freddie was impressed and admiringly watched as Enzo continued to dance around the ring, taking steps to move away from a would-be opponent and moving in to throw some combination punches. After a minute or two, he signaled he was ready for his sparring match.

Billy Blocker, a journeyman, and no stranger to Enzo, was his sparring mate again today. The single ring of the bell signaled the time for the round to begin, and both boxers moved in closer to each other. Enzo was the first to move in and fired several left jabs at Billy. One of the three found its mark and moved him back slightly. They continued to dance around, with both throwing some ineffective combination punches that were not at all damaging. Round one ended at the sound of the three rings of the bell, finding neither boxer showing any signs of being in a fight. The tempo picked up during round two with both boxers getting stung with effective right crosses. The final round was up-tempo and ended with Enzo inflicting four effective rights to Billy's body and a hard right cross to his head. His bobbing and weaving proved to be effective in avoiding punches aimed at him. As the boxers climbed down out of the ring, B.J. went over to Freddie and asked, "Well, champ, are you ready for some training in the boxing game?" In a halting voice he answered, "I don't believe I have what it takes to stand in and take the punishment Enzo's sparring mate did. I more than likely will be back here again to watch my friend perform. I enjoyed what I witnessed here today and liked the friendly atmosphere." "Wow, that is the first time somebody referred to my place as having a friendly atmosphere. I must be doing something wrong."

It was time for the two buddies to get on with the rest of their day. They freshened up somewhat and bid B.J. farewell, who shouted out a question for Freddie, "Have you ever been in the ring?" He replied without hesitation, "I told you I couldn't handle that kind of punishment."

They no sooner got out of the door when Freddie quizzically questioned Enzo, "What gave you the idea to start the day off at the gym?" He replied, "We are pretty close to Gertie's Hamburger Heaven, and I am famished. Let's finish the conversation while we eat. Have you ever been to Gertie's before?" "Hasn't everybody in Paducah? I have been there several times before and really enjoy the food, the service, and the low prices. I guess we pretty much share the same taste for food. Like two peas in a pod."

They arrived at their destination and were quickly greeted by Gertie with, "I hope you two brought your appetite with you. I need to be selling some food." Enzo quipped, "We might be buyers if you sell good food here." She came back with, "You rascal, you have never found anything to complain about on any of your visits." "I hope you don't give us anything to complain about today." "Your buddy there wouldn't complain even if there was a reason to do so. He is too much of a gentleman. I hope that some of him rubs off on you. Sit down before all the seats are filled and be quiet. I don't want you disturbing my fine guests." Enzo ended the conversation with, "And she charges for all that abuse, and us suckers keep coming back." She came back over to their table and greeted them with, "What will it be today, sweethearts?"

In a short amount of time their order was brought over to them and neither of them wasted any time getting down to the business of devouring some savory food. "About my question earlier. I'm anxious to hear your response." "There is a common thread that links us up. Our paths have crossed several times and for some reason I was interested in finding out why you were having a problem with securing a job. I was able to piece together the fact that you were involved in some fisticuffs that became the core of your problem. It was things I overheard, was told by another job seeker, and pieced together myself. You were a victim of circumstance. I, on the other hand, caused my problem. I am ashamed to say that I was caught stealing some sports equipment. You're probably wondering where we are linked by a common thread. I was a thief; you were a victim. Quite opposite situations, don't you think? Now, here is where the rub comes into play. We were purposely hired because of our predicaments. They are wanting to hire people who have had run-ins with the law, are having trouble finding work, and who seem to be easily manipulated. Does any of what I have said ring a bell with you? Has there been any happening or circumstance that poses a question to you?" Freddie was aghast and replied, "Do you know what, those are the kind of questions that have been floating around in my mind since I started at Swanson's. I still don't feel like it answers my question regarding your choice of the gym. Enzo explained further, "The fights you were involved in were not of your choice. You were responding to a bully in all of your encounters, according to what I have heard. Additionally, early on you were reluctant to defend yourself and were willing to absorb the punishment. Eventually, for whatever reason, you began to defend yourself and dish out some punishment to your adversaries. I go to the gym and spar around because it is enjoyable to me. I want to see how good I might be capable of becoming. I am not seeking to become a professional boxer; I know my limitations. I want to be in there to see how much punishment I am capable of absorbing. All the while, this is fun for me, and I enjoy doing it. I have no anger, have no desire to hurt anybody, and lastly it gives me confidence. I know that I will stand my ground if the need arises. I may not end up being the victor, but what I have learned will lessen my chances of becoming a victim. I feel it would be good for you for all of the reasons that I have mentioned. Plus, it would be fun to do this together." They noticed that there were people waiting to be seated. Freddie and Enzo vacated their seats so that Gertie could sell some more hamburgers. She flashed them a smile of appreciation and said, "You all come back now, you hear?" In unison they replied, "You can bet on that."

Once out the door, the conversation picked up from where they left off. Enzo was first to speak. "Freddie, I don't know about you, but I am not feeling too good about my employment status. I don't feel safe, and I am not trustful of too many of our fellow employees. Something is going on there that leads me to believe that the store is a front for a drug peddling operation. It appears that somebody in the organization is living two lives. The one that I could possibly see as being that person is Fred Gaines. I say that because of the many times I have seen a group in the Grocery Department that are definitely not employees. Why would Gaines allow for that to take place if he did not have ulterior motives for doing so? Another reason for feeling this way is because he was the first employee to be hired, and I have since found out that he was personally hired by Mr. Swanson. Mr. Swanson is not a native of Paducah, or of Kentucky for that matter. He came in here three years ago to buy a failing business in an old, dilapidated building. He poured a lot of money into remodeling the premises, and soon the business began to flourish. The store seems to be fairly well run, and there seems to be some very efficient employees on the payroll. Those facts do not lessen my suspicions though, neither about the business or of Fred Gaines. You probably think I may be off track in my thinking, and if so, do not hesitate to let me know." "I don't think that at all. As I have told you earlier, I have had some of the same thoughts as you. I must say though that your investigative work only makes me feel so much stronger that there is something going on that is not on the up and up. I guess the next question is what do we do to find out more and stay safe while doing that?" "If you are up to it, I would say that this next week should be spent observing and doing so without raising any suspicion. We will get together again next Saturday, and perhaps you might find interest in doing some training yourself. It may serve us well, should a need to protect ourselves arise. I trust you. Are you in on looking further into what is going on?" "You must know that I am one hundred percent in favor of doing just that."

It was nearing dinner time as they returned to their homes. Having reached their parting point in the route, they bid each other goodbye. Freddie's thoughts focused on the fact that he had finally found a job, one he was liking. But now he wondered if that was good fortune or not.

CHAPTER SIX:

THE PLOT THICKENS

Back at work it was business as usual. Freddie was engaged with an older couple who was disappointed that a product they had been seeking was still unavailable in the store. They reported they had made requests for the product on three different trips to the store. Freddie advised them to wait while he went to check if there was any back stock. Upon doing so, he again noticed what he had come to describe as "non-employees" gathered there. He made a quick glance over to see if he recognized any of them from previous occasions but had to pull away from his search as he was being eyed by several of the group. So as not to attract further attention to himself, and in keeping with what he and Enzo had decided about laying low, he started to leave. An associate approached him and asked him what he was looking for. When he informed him of what he was seeking, Freddie received an abrupt answer of, "No, there is none here." He was then rudely informed to seek out somebody instead of searching on his own. He promptly exited and returned to the customer service desk. Freddie assured the couple that he would personally put in a request for the product and that it should be delivered on next Tuesday's truck. He was thanked by the appreciative couple, who praised him for attending to their request for help in the matter.

In a span of about fifteen minutes, standing at the front of his desk was Fred Gaines. "Hey Pug, did you find what you were looking for? Being referred to as Pug, and the manner in which he was addressed was discomforting to Freddie. It took him a while to respond. Before he was able to compose himself Gaines directed a harsh, "Well?" at him. "No, I didn't, but I was helped by somebody who told me there was none in stock. "Let me tell you how you handle the situation in the future. One, you get on the phone and call me personally. Two, you don't come barging into my department for any reason at all. It seems I made a good decision when I refused to have you come to work for me. Need I say more? I am sure you won't be doing the wrong thing again."

The conversation between the two proved to be very disconcerting to Freddie and placed him in a contemplative mood. *How in the world did he learn of the handle that I had been tagged with?* Questions were weighing heavily on his mind. *What gave him pause to take such a combative attitude in regard to my innocent and non-threatening actions?*

Suddenly, Bruce Cannon appeared out of nowhere and quickly posed the question, "What was that exchange between you two all about?" "To tell the truth, I really don't know. I simply went into the grocery area to check to see if we had an item some customers were not able to find on the shelves. For whatever reason, my presence in Gaines' department troubled him. I didn't do anything that should have upset him so badly. I was not able to find an employee in the department and simply searched for the item I was trying to find." "Seems innocent enough to me. You didn't damage anything in the process, did you?" "No, I moved several cases in order to check what the bottom cases contained. I was extremely careful not to disturb anything, and I made sure to put it all back in place." Bruce quizzically replied, "I guess one never knows what will set a person off, does one? I wouldn't let it bother me, but here after, should you need help in such a matter, let me take care of it." The conversation ended with Freddie responding, "Gladly, and thanks for your concern."

His first order of business was to fill out an item request form for the product the customers were seeking. He promptly completed the form and placed it in the file tray assigned to the Grocery Department. He was ready for lunchtime to arrive and eager to fill Enzo in about today's happenings. After eating lunch in the employee break room, they took the time to walk about the store and talked in hushed tones. Freddie related what transpired earlier in the day. He brought him up to date about Bruce Cannon's intervention regarding the verbal exchange with Mr. Gaines. Enzo again cautioned him to lay low and not to attract any further attention to himself. "I guess it will require me to be constantly alert, even while in the performance of my job." "Yes, and speaking of jobs, it is time for us to get back to work. Lunch time is over. I'll call you later this evening."

Back at the service counter, he started thinking about how difficult it was going to be for him to get back into the pharmacy to check on those empty sample pill bottles. He was sure he had seen some bottles that were from Amber Laboratories. It was the firm that his dad represented. It had been several months since he was escorted through there when he first caught sight of them. He wondered if they

would still be around. His next thought was to figure out a
reason to be in there.

Freddie had just finished dinner and was in the process of
selecting the channel for tonight's Cubs baseball game when
he received the anticipated call from Enzo. They visited on
the phone for a prolonged time, conversing about the day's
activities they encountered after lunch. He had nothing to
report and found that Enzo did not have anything worth
mentioning. It was the third inning when they ended the call,
and he found that he had missed seeing back-to-back
homeruns hit by the Cub's number seven and eight batters.
He would have liked to have seen them but was more
interested in the call. They cemented their plans for
Saturday's outing, a much-desired event.

It was a slow Wednesday morning at the store and Freddie
was deep in thought about what they would be doing on
Saturday. That is, if it was to ever get here. A call came in for
him from Ms. Brooks,' requesting him to come to her office
upon getting his boss' permission. Ed had no problem with
him going right then. They would be fine given how slow
things were at the present time. He left and wandered off at a
slow pace observing all he could on the way. Ms. Brooks
greeted him but did not sound as enthusiastic as she was
while addressing him on the phone. She appeared to be
shaken, and he thought she might have been rubbing her
eyes. It did look like a tear had fallen across her cheek, which
she quickly wiped off.

"Freddie, I wanted to share some news with you that I thought you would like to hear. Do you recollect the incident you had with a couple looking for a bottle of Kitchen Bouquet the other day? Well, they were so impressed with the way you handled their request for help, they called to see if there was anything they could do for you. I informed them that our employees are expected to do exactly as you had done and are paid for the job they perform. I assured them that you would certainly appreciate the kind words and would not have expected any kind of reward. I am pleased to tell you that I had a word with Mr. Frye, and we both agreed that your work performance to date, along with your strong desire to please customers is worthy of a fifteen cent raise to be effective on your next pay period. It is rare that a raise is offered during an employee's probationary period, but I assure you that you have earned it." "Wow, I certainly did not expect this, I thank you and Mr. Frye for your kindness. Thank you so much." "Keep up the good work, it does not go unnoticed. Make sure you thank Mr. Frye when you get back to your department. Oh! By the way, do so in private. This is not to be discussed with fellow associates, or when they are nearby and able to overhear the conversation. Good luck to you."

Upon his return, he immediately sought out Ed Frye to do exactly as Ms. Brooks instructed him to do. While doing so, fellow employee, Toby, overheard the end of the conversation where Mr. Frye said, "Keep up the good work. There will be more good to come from it." He wondered just exactly what was the 'good' that came from it, and what was the good work that earned it. It was not like anything he had heard from Ed in the more than six months that he had been on the job. It seemed to him that ever since Freddie came on the scene, he had been relegated to the rear seat. Freddie had become the boss' favorite, and it was not to his liking.

The next morning found Ms. Brooks on the phone, not at all enjoying the conversation. The belligerent male caller spoke in a loud, offensive manner and belittled her in every imaginable way. "I was under the impression that you knew exactly what was expected of you. At first, I was under the illusion that you were actually fit for the job. Now I have great concerns about your ability, or should I say your lack of it. I found you a lawyer to get you out of a jail sentence, put you in a high paying position, and get nothing from you in return. That had better change, and in a hurry, or you will find yourself without a job. With your history, you will be hard pressed to find employment anywhere. You were told to hire people considered as being unemployable. That should not present a problem to you, or anybody else for that matter. I heard all the excuses from a dumb blonde that I care to hear. I have drugs that need to be sold before John Law gets any more aggressive and stifles our activity." "Sir, I have a balancing act to contend with. In the process of interviewing the types you want to be hired, I find they do not have the skills, let alone the common sense, to keep the grocery store operational. You said you needed the store to appear as a legitimate operation. That demands some functional people." "Right now, I need mules to move the drugs, and pushers to get them sold. I am rapidly losing patience with your ineptness and lack of action. Get the job done, or else." He slammed the phone down on the cradle, neglecting to say goodbye and adding to the pressure that she was under.

Ms. Brooks buried her face in her palms. *What have I got myself into? It would have been so easy to plead guilty to the charge against me and serve the probation time I was offered. Had I done that, I wouldn't be digging this deep hole that I seem to be putting myself in.* She reasoned that the bribe she took only helped one person. By pleading guilty she would have set him up for a charge that would have brought considerable jail-time. She knew her action set him free, and now he was a threat to her. Her guilty plea would have landed him in jail where he would unlikely be able to make good on his threats. She also would have had police protection. Now she faced a greater threat, possible to be carried out, and no protection or sympathy from the police at this time. A slick lawyer placed her in a time and place that made it impossible for her to have committed the crime she was being accused of. This enabled her to falsely testify that her threatener was with her that evening. The end result was that the police had no case against him.

CHAPTER SEVEN:

A BIT OF GOOD, BAD AND UGLY

It was seven days until the family would be celebrating Freddie's eighteenth birthday and Maureen was in a tizzy getting ready to host a party for him. There was shopping to do, a present to buy, a cake to be baked, along with all of the normal preparations for the impending celebration. Today was going to be the day for making telephone calls to invite the guests that would be attending. It was not a long list, and there would be no relatives attending due to the far distance they would have to travel. It was of great importance to her to make sure that Freddie's new friend, Enzo, would be able to attend. The others would be neighbors living in the same apartment complex as the one they inhabited. The rest of the week would be relegated to completing the remaining tasks in an orderly manner. She planned to have the party on Friday, that being his actual birthday, in order to leave Saturday, open for the boys' regular outing day. She had completed the list of things to do for the occasion when Freddie walked into the kitchen. He thanked her for the delicious breakfast she had prepared and informed her he was departing for the day. He would be back prior to six o'clock, in time for dinner.

He was off in his usual haste to arrive at their meeting place at the scheduled time. He arrived five minutes early and found Enzo present and warmly greeted him on his arrival. They wasted no time in heading off to their appointed destination. On arrival B.J. greeted them with, "Well, look what the cat dragged in, double trouble." Enzo answered, "Good morning to you too." B.J. queried, "Champ, are you putting the gloves on today?" Without hesitation Freddie quickly answered, "Now you surely know the answer to that question. Could I please have bag gloves so I can punish a speed bag?" "Sure, champ, anything for you." Enzo was entertained with the back and forth between the two of them and got ready for his usual warm-up routine before his sparring match. While Enzo was busy prepping, Freddie tapped away at the bag, and his tempo set off a very pleasing sound to B.J. The fact was it drew all of his attention. He sure liked what he was hearing and seeing. "Hey, champ, save some of those punches for a stint in the ring today." "B.J., you are sure one persistent aggravator. And you are also hard of hearing it seems. Is that a result of too much ring time for you?" "Wow, the champ is as fast with his tongue as he is with his hands. Touche." "Hey Enzo, the old guy is a French linguist." The whole gym burst out with laughter. Enzo chimed in with, "You two should put the gloves on."

Enzo was ready for his sparring partner to step in and was going through his usual footwork routine. It was not Billy Blocker that he would be matched up with today. Instead, it was a younger fellow with whom he was not familiar. They touched gloves, returned to their respective corners, and waited for the bell. Round one got off to somewhat of a flurry as a lot of leather was thrown by the new guy. None of the punches were damaging, but it appeared that they aggravated Enzo a bit. It might be said that they probably bothered Freddie a lot more. He went over to Enzo's corner and told him to stay away from the guy as much as he possibly could. Use a peek-a-boo defensive mode when he comes in on you, and then drop your hands and prepare to defend against quick body punches. The bell sounded for round two and his corner's advice was well heeded, enabling Enzo to ward off some well thrown punches from his opponent. He did manage to land two very well-placed right crosses that jarred the young lad quite a bit. In the corner between rounds, Freddie told him to carry the fight now. "Come out and take a defensive stance for a short period than go on the attack, move in on him and look for whatever opening he presents." His combatant assumed Enzo had exhausted himself and decided he would bring the fight to him. He came in fast, and Enzo switched modes and caught him with a stiff left, followed by an explosive right hand that quickly ended the match. Freddie was grinning from ear to ear and was certainly pleased with Enzo's one-two punch finish to the match. B.J. was in disbelief of Enzo's performance and more so in Freddie's corner advice that brought about the change in Enzo's fighting style. B.J. questioned, "Hey champ, was that you in the ring fighting the last two rounds?" "No, I could never be as good as the guy that just put on such a marvelous performance." It was time to depart and get on with the rest of the day's plans.

The trip from the gym led them on the route that would carry them over to Gertie's place again. They arrived on the scene and seeing the crowd waiting to get in to be served, they made a decision to try somewhere else for lunch. Neither of them was able to suggest where they might try to go for a quick bite. They were both of the opinion that wherever they would go, the food would not be as good as it would have been at Gertie's. Enzo suggested, "I know of an old Greek restaurant that I have eaten at on several occasions that we might try. It's not in the best part of town, but the food is worth the trip. I think you will probably agree with me. You might like Souvlaki or perhaps a Gyro Sandwich. They have the best Gyro I have ever eaten." "Oh! Did you say Gyros? We'd better hurry. You have me drooling already."

Fifteen hurried minutes later they arrive at the Papadakis Brothers Bistro. When Enzo said it was old, he wasn't kidding. It looked like it might have been built about the same time as the Acropolis. Once inside it didn't matter what it looked like. The aroma of the food being cooked took front and center attention. It was what mattered most. They were there to eat the food, not to admire architecture. Halfway into the meal, Freddie uttered the first words spoken, "Man, Enzo, I'm not sure I want to go back to Gertie's now that I have eaten here. I love these Gyro's. They're great." "Yeah, champ, I know. By the way, do you happen to recognize any of that group of four guys occupying the back booth on the right side?" "No, not really, I haven't been focusing on them, or haven't you noticed?" "Oh, I noticed alright. I was wondering if you were going to take time to breathe in between bites." "Ha ha, and what is this champ bit?" Enzo questioned, "Does the word bother you?" "No not really, I just don't think it's appropriate." "Well, you better get used to it, you had the whole gym buzzing after my match today." "They were buzzing alright, and it was because of your performance. I wasn't the one throwing the leather around. It happened to be you, and you did it masterfully." Enzo again, "Yes and it was done as a result of your knowledgeable instructions while acting as my cornerman." "So, the guy sitting in the corner not taking nor throwing punches is to get all the credit? Is that how it works? It's no wonder I don't want to get into the ring. I don't want to become a punching bag for a guy who thrives on beating the daylights out of somebody, anybody." "I get that, but the thing about it, Freddie, is that you would not allow them to do that to you. You're too smart and savvy to let that happen." Freddie interrupted the conversation and asked Enzo, "Are you ready for some fresh air and sunshine?" "You bet, buddy, let's do it."

They got up to depart, and the foursome Enzo was questioning him about got up to leave at the same time. While doing so, one of the four made it a point to intercept them and violently elbowed Enzo. Freddie aggressively stepped in between them, and begged the question, "What is this all about? We haven't bothered any of you." A reply from the elbow-thrower informed him to butt out, as this was none of his concern. "Oh, but it is, this is my friend, and I won't stand here and allow this to continue." Enzo blurted out, "I am not going to allow it either. Now if you don't get out of our way, I will put you out of our way. Move over, we are coming through." It turned out to be advice well heeded by the troublemaker, and they moved on to their next venture for the day.

Enzo inquired, "Freddie, did you recognize any of them?" "I do believe I had seen one of them in the Grocery Department at the store. I can't be totally sure, but he did look familiar to me." As they moved on, Freddie had to conceal his smile and the admiration he had for his loyal friend that day. They had developed a strong bond, one which would serve them well into the future. They spent the rest of the day doing things that they enjoyed. The time came to call it a day and to offer parting remarks. The final exchange came from Freddie when he offered, "So long, champ. I'm glad to have you as a friend. See you tomorrow."

CHAPTER EIGHT:

TIME TO REFLECT

Another Monday morning and a very bleak one at that
arrived, with low hanging clouds spitting a light drizzle down
on the Paducah area. The lack of sunshine was especially
unwelcome to one Gloria Brooks who was in a deep
depression. She found herself ruminating about her present
predicament. Her thoughts seemed to be bouncing off the
walls and flying back at her like a Boomerang, and there was
no stopping it. They kept coming back. She wondered how in
the world she got herself into this mess. Ms. Brooks recalled
that chance meeting, several dates, and then that fateful
evening when her world turned upside down. She had no idea
of the stop he would make, nor the reason for it. The next
day she found the reason for the stop from a police officer
who had knocked on her door at a very early hour of the
morning. He advised her of her rights and told her to get
dressed for a trip to the nearby Station. Gloria was
bewildered about the proceedings but would soon find out
that she was being named as an accomplice in a drug drop.
Not a run-of-the-mill drop, but rather one valued at a million
dollars. She was flabbergasted. She was not guilty of any
wrongdoing. Gloria had no part in it nor had any knowledge
about it.

The next thing she knew, the officer interrogating her put her on the defensive. He had insisted that she was an accomplice in the matter, and he wanted an admission of guilt. Gloria was not guilty of anything, and she wanted to talk to her lawyer. And then she thought, *what lawyer? I don't have a lawyer.* Suddenly, she remembered getting a card from her date, and him telling her if she ever needed legal representation, to call the number on the card. Gloria did just that. She never would have thought she would be in need of a lawyer.

The supposed lawyer showed up and looked more like somebody who needed a lawyer himself. She was not impressed or thrilled by the fact that he would be the one to represent her in the matter. She certainly did not have a choice of someone else, and besides, she could not afford a lawyer. It was what it was. He questioned her to determine what was exchanged between her and the interrogator. He proceeded to tell Gloria that she should plead not guilty. She assured him she had already made them aware of that. He advised her, "From now on, your response will be that you were with him the entire time. The two of you were at Tootsies' Lounge, and we have three witnesses, plus a barmaid and a bartender, that will attest to that." Gloria advised him that she could not do that. "You have no choice in the matter." "I do not want to face a perjury charge." "I will not allow you to perjure yourself." He assured her that she was not doing anything that would allow for a charge of perjury. "I am here to protect you in every way. You either do that or you will be facing a guilty plea and be convicted." She insisted that she would not be a part of what he was planning to do. He told her if she did not, she would be faced with all costs associated with the trial from whoever was representing her and would not receive twenty-five thousand dollars from him for doing her part. He asked if she was going to do as he was suggesting, in order to be judged innocent of the charge, have no record, and be a bit richer. She conceded to do as he requested. After he had finished informing her how to proceed, they were rejoined by the police and stated their position. Soon after, she was released. Before they parted, she told him she no longer had a job at the Middle School and needed help in securing new employment. "That will be taken care of for you. I will be in touch. You talk to no one, give no comments to anyone. If approached, call me immediately. Good-bye for now."

She was exhausted from all of these thoughts and knew she had to clear her mind now. She had no desire to continue on thinking about what transpired in that exchange. She also did not want to contemplate what the future had in store for her.

Enzo was busy freshening up the fruit displays and was feeling the effects of some of the body blows he was subjected to on Saturday. It seemed that today required more freshening than was usual on Monday's past. There had to be a rush on business over the weekend accounting for that fact. He figured one might know it would be the case when he was a bit more banged up. The last thing he wanted was to become a punching bag for someone again. He was ready for lunch and some friendly conversation with Freddie.

Up at the service counter, Freddie was confronted with an emergency situation presented by a customer who had a bad cut on her hand. She was not even aware as to when or where it happened, but the sight of blood sure got her attention. She requested some assistance from a customer who escorted her over to Freddie. He quickly wrapped a clean towel over the wound and hurried her over to the pharmacy area. He figured they had the items needed to deal with the emergency and had some medical knowledge that would be useful in dealing with her wound. One of the pharmacists recognized there was a problem requiring some attention and came out to help. "Let's get you inside the pharmacy and get you off your feet so I can determine the course of action. It does not appear that the cut will require stitches, but we need to stop the bleeding. I will apply butterfly stitches to close up the wound." The druggist had the situation well in hand within a matter of ten minutes or so. The lady was asked if she was in pain and acknowledged she had none at all. She also said she did not need any further help and was ready to go about completing her shopping. The druggist turned to draw Freddie's attention, who had moved to the back aisle. He called out to him, and upon his return, questioned his absence from the area where the lady was being treated. Freddie explained, "The sight of blood got to me, and I needed to get away to settle myself down. I was afraid that I might faint." The druggist did not feel Freddie had the appearance of someone who might have been affected that way. "Alright, we are done here, you can escort the lady out and see to her further needs, if any."

He finished assisting the lady and felt very uneasy about how things ended with the druggist who had aided her. He thought he might have been suspicious of his actions. Freddie had his own suspicions. *I didn't see the empty pill bottles from my dad's company, but it seemed like none of the others had been moved.*

Thursday morning found Maureen completing preparations for the big celebration on Friday evening. The invitations had been sent out, all of the grocery shopping was completed, and now she was going about doing what was necessary to put her best foot forward. She wanted this to be the best birthday that Freddie had experienced. The family's slush fund, used for emergency needs, was raided to purchase his first watch. She hoped that he would be as pleased with it as she was. It meant so much to her that this celebration was to be perfectly planned and enjoyed by all.

CHAPTER NINE:

HAPPY BIRTHDAY

Store owner, Mr. Swanson, was at his desk early Friday morning when he was startled by the ringing of his telephone. *Who could be calling at this hour when the store doesn't open until almost two hours from now?* The caller greeted him, "Carl, good morning to you, I have some good news. I found an empty building in Marion that would serve you perfectly in furthering your expansion plans. The building is larger than your present location and is in much better condition. Even better news is that the owner is hard pressed for cash at the present time and is a very eager seller. Two options are available, rent to own, or purchase outright immediately. The rent is a bargain, but I do believe purchasing the property is the way to go. I don't think it would take much to talk the seller down on his asking price, knowing his present need for cash. I can meet you in Marion at noon for lunch and we can check out the location and get started on all of the details. Are you able to make it this afternoon? If so, say the word and I will be there. We can meet at the location whose address is 1235 Victoria Street. You will love the area. There is not a single empty store to be seen, and the traffic is never ending. I suggest you give your immediate attention to the matter. It won't stay on the market very long. You do not want to miss a good deal when it is staring you in the face."

"I had plans to take off this afternoon to take a run over to Carbondale to look at a property that is up for sale. I guess I can meet you at noon, and if your location turns out to be such a good deal, I will forsake going over to Carbondale. I think the economy is at a place at this time that will make it easy for me to make the decision when the ideal location comes available. I'll be there at noon, Rocco, see you then."

Lunch time found the two buddies, Enzo and Freddie, off on their lunch break enjoying the relaxation and their time together. Enzo said, "I just heard about your experience with the lady and her bad cut. You did not by any chance get to snooping around while you were in the pharmacy?" "Not exactly." "Not exactly? I know precisely what that means. Do you want to tell me the whole story?" "Well, I saw an opportunity to go to the back area and found that what I was looking for was no longer there." "And that was?" "The pill bottles that bore the labels from my dad's company. I wonder why his were gone and the others remained there. It does not seem right to me." Enzo replied, "It is a bit strange, but I don't really see how it can turn into a problem for you. Did anybody notice you being back there?" "Yeah, the druggist that helped with bandaging up the lady's hand." "And?" "He did appear to show concern about the fact I had done so." With a big sigh, Enzo replied, "I am sure glad you are laying low, and following my advice. Are you looking forward to your birthday tomorrow? In case we don't get to have lunch together tomorrow, I will see you on Saturday. Keep a low profile, will you?"

Friday was a whirlwind day at work. Besides being busy all day, the department held a little celebration for the birthday boy. They managed to find time for a piece of cake that was baked for the occasion. He was excited and grateful to his fellow employees and made certain that each one was personally thanked for the good wishes they offered. He was bothered that he had not seen Enzo, who had not made any attempt to see him. *He knows well it is my birthday today.*

Another workweek was over with and found Freddie on his way home performing the same tasks that were his normal routine. He still was bothered by the lingering fact that his buddy did not wish him a happy birthday. *Perhaps tomorrow he has something planned.*

He arrived home, opened the door, and was greeted by a thunderous recital of Happy Birthday, and the smiling face of his friend, Enzo. The appearance of his loving mother, his dutiful father, faithful friend Enzo, and his favorite neighbors had made his day. It was definitely the time to celebrate birthday number eighteen. The presence of one Mary Lee Bancroft was a pleasing and surprising treat. It surely would be numbered among his lasting memories. The time Maureen looked forward to most was when she and Conor would present Freddie with his first watch. After dining on some hot hors d'oeuvres, and the delicious cake that she had baked, she invited everyone to join in singing HAPPY BIRTHDAY, which was rendered in a somewhat off-key manner. It wasn't the sound that mattered, it was the well-wishes that he received and appreciated. It was time to present the watch.

Freddie was emotional and choked up for joy. He could hardly muster the words to thank his thoughtful parents. A few other small gifts from the guests were opened along with Enzo's gift of a one-year membership to B.J.'s gym. This was certainly a night to be remembered.

Mr. Swanson and Rocco had their afternoon visit which culminated in plans to offer to purchase the property for cash. An amount below the asking price was offered and hopefully would be acceptable to the present owner. Rocco figured the owner's need for cash would be reason for him to jump on the deal without any hesitation. Carl was wondering if he would be able to muster the full amount needed, and when informing Rocco of his concern, he was told that it would not be a problem. Rocco had access to whatever cash would be needed to seal the deal. "You know we are willing and able to satisfy your needs, and we expect you to do the same for us. It was not too long ago that you were down and out and now you are doing alright for yourself. That will be the case in the future as long as you play ball with us. That's not going to become a problem for you, is it?" Carl answered, "I see no reason for it to become a problem." He was convinced he would not be borrowing any money from Rocco's source ever again.

The following day, the two, joined at the hip friends met, and promptly scurried over to B.J.'s gym, where they were warmly greeted by none other than the illustrious owner of the number one-rated gym in Paducah. It was not that much of a prestigious honor since his was the only gym in the city. B.J., though, was quite proud to have the honor bestowed on the gym and basked in the glory. It didn't matter that he was the grantor of the title. "Well, ladies, what did I do to deserve your company this fine morning?" Enzo quipped, "Not a thing, you never do. Can we get down to business, and officially welcome the new member to this hopefully up-and-coming business?" B.J. asked, "Just exactly what is that supposed to mean?" "You're the brains behind this outfit, you'll figure it out." Scratching his head and totally confused with the last remark, he got down to business. "Welcome, champ, I am glad to have you as a member. You are a fine addition to our little world. I am happy that you are joining us, and I thank Enzo for his generosity that made it possible." Enzo chimed in, "Will you look at that, the place is already starting to show some class, keep it up B.J."

They got ready for the day's activity and Enzo reminded Freddie that he had access to all the services the gym offered and asked him what he was planning for his first day's routine." "He had no answer to the question and replied, "I really have no idea as to where to start. I am not sure what I intend to achieve. I am going to need some help." "That is what B.J. is here for. He can get you started on a regimen and leave it up to you to set your pace, and also determine if you are heading in a direction that serves your purpose. You have a whole year to figure that out."

In short order, B.J. and Freddie got their heads together and were setting up a routine for him to follow. During that time B.J. availed himself of the opportunity to inform Freddie that

he had the makings of a good boxer, if that was of interest to him. If that was what he wanted, he would do everything possible to help him achieve success. "What I have observed so far in the several weeks that you have been coming here is that you are gifted. You have what none of the others here possess. You are like a rough gem waiting to be cut, polished, and made ready to sparkle. I have a strong feeling that, if you developed the desire, your light would shine brightly. I am at your disposal. You tell me when you want my help."
"Thanks, B.J., I am going to take it slow and feel my way around. I appreciate your kind words as well as your offer to help me. I will not hesitate to take advantage of your apt assistance if the spirit moves me in that direction. I am not inclined that way at the present time."

Both of them worked up a sweat and a hearty appetite for some good vittles and proceeded to head toward Pappadakis Bistro again. Freddie knew that his choice for the day was going to be Soutzouki because he favored veal. He enjoyed his selection considerably. They indulged in some Baklava and Greek almond cookies, more than they should have, and departed heavier than when they arrived. It could be said of both of them that they left well satisfied. Enzo remarked, "We go to the gym, lose unwanted pounds, and a half hour later we put them all back on."

As they departed, Enzo asked Freddie, "What do you say we take a walk down to the riverfront? I haven't been down to the river in quite some time. I enjoy going there, it is so peaceful at times. Are you up for it?" Freddie was in deep thought and failed to respond in a timely manner, garnering a "where are you" from Enzo. "Oh sorry, I was thinking that

the quilting museum was located near there, and that it would
be a nice place to take my mother. Sorry about that. Yes, I'm
all in to head down to the riverfront. I have only been there
one time since moving here and did not spend a whole lot of
time taking in the sights." The rest of their afternoon together
was spent walking and discussing plans for the following
Saturday. They stuck to their usual plan and decided they
would have lunch at one of the restaurants in the area after
finishing their workouts at B.J.'s gym. Freddie noted, "I am
really looking forward to that, I sure hope we have another
nice day like today." The time to end the day's outing had
arrived, and the two of them started on their homeward trek.
Goodbye's and wishes for a good rest of the weekend were
exchanged as they reached the split-up point.

He was greeted with a, "My you are home early today" from
his mother, who was anxiously awaiting his arrival. "Did you
boys have a great day?" "We sure did, we spent a good part
of five hours walking around down by the river. We need to
take a trip to the Quilting Museum, and then go down to the
riverfront and have dinner one Sunday." "Oh! I would really
love to do that. Would you be willing to make that happen
tomorrow?" "I sure would, we need to get Dad on board. I
can't think of anything else that I would rather do. Enzo said
there are several good restaurants to choose from. He named
one, but I can't remember the name right now. It will come
to me when we are in the area."

Conor arrived a bit later, said he had a good sales day, and
added he was sure glad to be home. He was in agreement to
make tomorrow the day for the riverfront outing. "I have

wanted to suggest we do that for some time now, but never got around to making it happen."

Sunday morning found the Ryan family rising earlier than usual to get ready for church services. They were greeted with a most beautiful day, featuring a warm balmy breeze, blue skies, and abundant sunshine. They would have to be considered very fortunate because this was not the norm for that time of year. Maureen had breakfast ready so they would not have to hurry and scurry in order to be on time for the early service.

Reverend George Turner kept everyone's attention with his compelling sermon about one's duty to take care of his fellow man. He was an exceptional speaker but seemed to be even more so on this particular day. The subject found Freddie reflecting on an old gentleman whose path he crossed yesterday. *I wonder if he has ample food and a safe place to stay.* Maureen's thoughts went to a member of her quilting club that could not afford the yarn she required to finish the quilt on which she was working. Conor was not at all absorbed in the subject matter being discussed and seemed to be in a different world. Something was bothering him greatly.

After the church service and on the way to their planned destination Maureen questioned, "Did today's sermon evoke any thoughts or incidents that troubled you?" Freddie was quick to answer, "I was bothered about an old man I had seen while Enzo and I walked the riverfront yesterday. I was disturbed by the fact that I felt he did not appear to be in a good spot in his life." "Why was that?" questioned Maureen. "It appeared to me that he was carrying all the possessions that he owned in this world. His face bore the expression of a person beaten down, and his eyes never made an attempt to look over to us as he passed by. His plight really concerned me, but what bothered me the most was that I had nothing to offer him to help improve his life. Enzo and I kind of splurged on food yesterday. Maybe a kind word from us might have helped him through his day." "Conor, how about you, anything cross your mind?" questioned Maureen. "Reverend Turner's sermon was disconcerting to me; I do not like to hear of or see people down and out." Freddie wanted to know, "What can we as a family do about it?" Maureen quickly added, "That is going to be our topic of discussion at dinner this week. Now we are going to enjoy our day out."

They arrived and decided that they would take advantage of the beautiful weather, do the walking and sightseeing now, and grab a bite to eat when they felt exhausted. About two hours into their day, they came across a group of young men. One of them addressed Conor, "Sir, how did you make out at Pete's Pool Palace yesterday? Those guys seemed to be very intimidating towards you." "I think you are mixed up; you have the wrong guy." "Oh no sir, I remember you very distinctly, you were wearing a light jacket with the name of a company above the breast pocket. It was Amber Laboratories." "They were not a threat to me. I knew one of the fellows. I had to see him about some repairs I wanted him to take care of." "My buddies and I were worried about your well-being."

"Dad, what is going on? Why were you at a pool hall? Why didn't you say something about being there to Mom and me last evening? Who are these guys that are intimidating you?" "Son, as I had just explained, I had repairs at the office needing to be done. Clarence could not get a ride over there, so I had to meet him at Pete's place." The young man intervened and said, "I remember you addressing the repair man as Rocco. He sure was not dressed like any repair person I had seen before. I am sorry to have to contradict you, but I do believe it is in the best interest of your wife and son to know the specific details. Ma'am, I will be glad to offer you my personal information should you require any further help my friends and I might be able to offer." One of the others in the group added, "I remember the guy being addressed as Rocco also. I did not hear his retort to you, but it seemed to have a threatening tone to it." Maureen politely thanked the boys and said she would definitely be in touch should a need to do so arise. She addressed Conor and Freddie saying, "I think it best we end the day here and head back to the apartment. I believe we have a lot to talk about and a restaurant is not the place for the conversation."

A somber forty minutes later found them back to the security of their abode where they continued on with the conversation. Maureen offered, "Conor, I do believe that you are in some sort of trouble. We want to help. In order for us to do so we need to know all of the facts surrounding your predicament. We love you and we need you. We don't want any harm to come to you, nor do we want you to be facing an incident that will be problematic for you. The more we know, the better we might be able to help." "Dad, I am overly concerned about the people you were dealing with at the pool hall. Please let us get involved so we can offer some help, no matter what little that could be."

"Do you remember telling me about a run-in you had with Bruno Balicki several months ago? I remember you saying that you were bothered from some of the blows he dealt that day. You further stated that neither of you felt like you were the winner in that confrontation. Does any of this bring back a recollection of that happening?" Freddie nodded affirmatively and Conor continued on with the discussion. Shortly after your altercation, I was visited by the senior Balicki who sought some help from me. He requested that since I was in pharmaceutical sales, could I possibly give him some painkillers to relieve his son's headaches. He claimed the headaches were a result of that fight. I told him that we are not responsible for any consequence that may have resulted. I advised him since it was Bruno who initiated the action, my son was compelled to protect himself. He agreed and asked if I could see to being a good neighbor and help this one time. Should I refuse to oblige and satisfy his needs there would be serious consequences forthcoming. I didn't dare refuse after hearing what might happen. I resisted at first, but finally conceded to offer two sample pill bottles of a pain reliever. It was against company policy, and my better judgement to do so. Now I am being threatened because I refused to supply a drug dealer with the pills I had given to Bruno's father. I have received several threats and have noticed some unsavory characters pacing up and down in front of the house. The threats are now being extended to your mother and you. I was warned that if I were to go to the police, the threats to you and your mother would become a reality. I don't know how to respond. I have been thinking about going to the police and requesting police protection. I'm afraid of being arrested for involvement in the matter. I am confused, worried, and upset about the whole situation."

CHAPTER TEN:

WHY US, LORD?

There was a dreaded gloom hanging over the Ryan household that Monday morning, none of which had to do with the weather in Paducah, Kentucky that fine day. Maureen, as well as Freddie, had no idea as to where to turn to furnish help of any kind or even where to begin. Conor was intent on coming up with a plan that would require police involvement. He was afraid, though, of what the consequences might be for Maureen and Freddie should the police fail to provide adequate protection for his loved ones. Before leaving to go to work he invited them to sit and listen to what he was planning to do. He wanted them to know that if he were to do as he was planning, it would leave them vulnerable to possible harm. Without hesitation, they both heartily agreed that he was taking the proper route to secure resolution. They were behind him one hundred percent and were there to help in any way they could.

The plan was to be discussed at the evening meal in order for everyone to be on the same page. Conor departed for work and Freddie was off to his place of employment. Maureen settled down to familiarize herself with all that had been presented thus far. She was going to learn as much as she could, and to figure out what other sources she could turn to for information or help. She had spent a good part of the morning pondering whatever crossed her mind. As she was getting ready to prepare a light lunch for herself, she was interrupted by the ringing of the phone. "Hello, this is Maureen. How can I help you?" "Ma'am, you don't know me. Allow me to introduce myself to you. I am Helen Suskind. My son and several of his friends crossed your family's path yesterday and informed me of what they had determined might be a problem for your family. If you are interested in what I have to say, I would be happy to continue conversing with you." "I would be more than happy to hear what you have to offer." "Fine then, we want to help as much as we can. The boys felt that your husband was not allowing you to know what a dangerous predicament with which he was faced. They told me that they overheard some terrible threats handed to him. They did not want to create a family breach by passing this information on to you and your son yesterday afternoon. They came to me to determine if they had done the right thing, and what steps needed to be taken to help. I can assure you that these boys are very sensible, highly intelligent, and very sensitive. They had the presence of mind to arrange for a picture of their group to be taken of them. It was taken in such a manner that it allowed for the intimidators faces to be completely disclosed in the photograph. They did it covertly and did not raise any suspicion of what they were accomplishing. I told you these are intelligent young men. I have taken the liberty to have the photos developed and enlarged, and I assure you they are noticeably clear and present recognizable facial features. Are you in a position to come and get the photos?" "I am not, but my husband would be able to pick them up. Where does he need to go to get them?" Mrs. Suskind suggested he come to her house, and he could do so at his convenience. "My address is 18 Kidlington Court. We are the third house on your right as you turn down our street. Our hearts and well wishes are with your family. Please be aware that we are here to help should you need it." "Helen, if I may refer to you as such, thank you from the bottom of my heart. You could not imagine how much your help is needed and appreciated at this time. I will have my husband, Conor, call before coming to pick up the photos. I would like to add that we all must treat this as a highly dangerous situation. The boys must not talk to anyone about anything. I am concerned for their safety." "I assure you the boys have been forewarned, and they have all sworn to secrecy. I am confident that they will be very discreet regarding the situation. They have been advised to be alert and to inform us parents in the event they feel threatened. I failed to say that they were told by us not to go anywhere near the pool hall." "Helen, I cannot thank you and the boys enough for the concern you have all shown and for all the help you have offered. Goodbye for now. Stay safe."

A sense of comfort overtook Maureen as she set about to prepare the evening meal. There was a deep feeling of appreciation for the help she had received from the boys' families. Maureen was most grateful for the concern that the young boys had shown for Conor's wellbeing. The photos that were so wisely taken were a start to building up a defense for Conor. Her emotions were running wild within her, and she was coming to the realization that there was a long hill to climb before the Ryan family would have real peace again.

Freddie came home and excitedly questioned, "Mom, what have you learned today? Are you doing alright? Any luck in finding out anything?" "Yes, Freddie, we are fortunate that there are neighborly citizens out there who are concerned about our wellbeing. Before I proceed to inform you as to what I have learned, I want you to settle down and take a deep breath. I have come to the conclusion that we have to rein in our emotions so that we expend our energies on clear thinking. I also want you to be aware of the gravity of our predicament. This could possibly erupt into a dangerous situation. All that we learn, as well as the plans that we make, have to remain inside these walls. The time will come when we feel confident about what our next steps should be."

"The four young boys who came to us because of their concern for your father's predicament have turned out to be wise beyond their age. They had the intelligence and foresight to take several photos and did so without drawing attention to what they wanted to accomplish. It turns out that one of the mothers called to inform me about picking up the pictures. She said that the photos clearly display the facial features of all of the people that intimidated your father. Your dad has arranged to stop at the home of Mrs. Suskind, the mother of two of the boys who are helping us. Now why don't you get spruced up for dinner? I will fill you and your dad in on the other information when we are all together. That will spare me from having to be repetitious when he is with us."

Freddie and Maureen were awaiting Conor's arrival and spent some time reflecting on their earlier discussion. They were overly anxious to see the photos and to be filled in on whatever plans Conor had formulated. They consumed their dinner in a quickened pace so they could get down to business. Maureen was the first to speak, inquiring of Conor, "Were you able to get the photographs?" "Yes, Mrs. Suskind was a wonderful person. I interrupted their dinner and was invited to join them. I, of course, informed her that you would have dinner waiting for me when I returned home. We spent a sizable amount of time with introductions and going over the photos. They could not have been more hospitable. I felt like I was dealing with friends we had known over our lifetime. I didn't want their food to get cold, so I did my best to depart quickly, but not before I offered my gratitude and to pay for the cost of the photos. They would not hear of it, and I thanked them again for their kind efforts. I parted, letting them know that we would like to have them as guests as soon as we were free to do so. They were quick to say that they would like that, but they felt we had enough to contend with presently. Helen and her husband told me that they were available to help if the need should arise. She ended by saying, 'We will be there for you whenever we can offer help. Do not hesitate to call regarding any matter.'"

Conor admitted that he really did not have plans to offer other than he was determined to go to the Police Station. He would relate he had supplied a small amount of sample pill bottles containing pain medication. He would let them know the facts surrounding his involvement, and how it came about. They would be made aware of the threats he had been receiving and how they have become more frequent and foreboding. They would be told that they were now aimed at harming his family. Conor was planning to request police protection but had no idea whether they would grant any. He did believe they were going to need it. He insisted that Maureen and Freddie go stay with her brother in Franklin, Tennessee until this mess was cleared up. "I do not want any harm to come to you two. That could possibly come as soon as they become aware that I have had a visit with the police." "Dad, I have a job. I don't want to lose it." Maureen added,

"Conor, I have no intention of leaving either of you. Plus, they may not become aware of your going to the police." Conor responded, "That very well may be the case, but that does not stop them from continuing to threaten us, or worse yet, to carry it out." Maureen added, "I, for one, will make no moves until you meet with the police and know what their plan of action is going to be." "Alright, it's settled then. I will go to the police the first thing tomorrow." Maureen interjected, "No, *we* will go to the police the first thing tomorrow. It will not be the Police Station where we will meet. I will set the time and the place. This will be done very discreetly so that we do not take the chance of being observed by anyone."

At the same time in the home of Hal and Helen Suskind at 18 Kidlington Circle, a conversation regarding the same matter was taking place. The children had already retired for the evening and Hal wanted to avail himself of the opportunity to have a private talk with his dear wife, Helen. He requested her full attention and said, "Helen, I believe we may be opening ourselves up to problems we do not want to have. What we have done so far in helping Mr. Ryan leaves us with the possibility of becoming involved. What we are offering in the way of our help will definitely place us in harm's way. When I say "we," it is to include us along with our two boys. It is enough for you and me to become entangled, but it is not what I relish for the boys. It is my opinion that we need to back off a bit." "Hal, you need to place our family in the predicament they are facing. Would you want someone to back off from helping us? We will talk with the boys, who are already aware of the danger involved, and seek their opinion as to our future involvement. Should the answer be to continue offering assistance we will proceed with extreme caution, and not do anything to draw attention. I would suspect that our contributions to the case will require close scrutiny by the police, who will most likely be concerned for our safety. I feel it is our duty to do all we can to help a neighbor and to eliminate the danger the drug pushers are creating. I hope that you find a way to feel as I do about the situation. Sleep on it, if you must, and we will finalize the decision tomorrow." "I don't need more time to decide. I am in complete accord with the way you feel." "Okay then, tomorrow we will get the boy's reaction in regard to our next steps."

CHAPTER ELEVEN:

SEEKING ANSWERS

The next day, it seemed, was not to go in a favorable manner in their pursuit of ferreting out what was what and who was who at the Supermarket. Enzo greeted Freddie early in the morning with his feeling that something was brewing, though he could not get a handle on what it was. "Freddie, I think we both need to be on high alert as to what transpires today. Keep a low profile while poking around, don't get too inquisitive. I do not like the feeling that has been with me since coming to work. I feel as if there are eyes focused on me. I have noticed Toby conversing with several different associates ever since I arrived. I have never felt this way before." "And I have never seen you so concerned about anything. Just know that I will play it safe and not get involved in anything at all today. I will keep my eyes and ears open though." "Good, champ, I'll see you at lunch."

Lunch came and went with the two of them sharing conversation while eating. Upon finishing, they both headed back to their respective departments. Enzo, on his return, was greeted by two employees he recognized as buddies of Toby. They shared pleasantries and he was asked if he would like to join them after work. He felt they had extended a sincere invitation which he could not accept. "Maybe another day," he replied. About the same time Toby and another friend of his met Freddie. Toby made a move appearing to extend a friendly gesture. Freddie responded in a like manner, allowing Toby to make it look as if he was knocked to the ground. His friend yelled out in a loud voice, "Hey, he didn't do anything to you. Why did you knock him down?" It was done in a loud, questioning manner and attracted several other employees. One of the nearby department managers came over to question the action. All of the employees on the scene attested that Freddie had initiated the action. The manager told Freddie he needed to come with him to Ms. Brooks' office. The other employees were advised to return to their departments, and not to comment on what had happened.

Ms. Brooks was apprised of the matter and was told that Toby complained of his shoulder hurting. Albert also informed her he did not see what took place. He did say that three witnesses to the incident had declared that Freddie was the antagonist. "Ms. Brooks, if there is nothing else you require of me, I need to return to my department." "Thank you, Albert, I appreciate your help. You are free to go. I may need you later, in which case I will contact you."

"Freddie, do you have anything to say for yourself?" "Yes ma'am, I do. I can honestly tell you that I did nothing to hurt Toby. It was a staged act to make it look as if I engaged him in a fight." "How does one account for the testimony provided by the three witnesses?" "Well, actually there was only one person besides Toby and me present that could have seen the goings-on. He was a part of the act and helped in setting me up. The other two were would-be observers that were staged to be available on signal. The signal being the loud outcry from the actor involved in the plot." Ms. Brooks went on to say, "I will tell you this, I have no doubt that what you are saying is the absolute truth. I want you to know that my hands are tied in the matter due to the accounts of the eyewitnesses. I have no alternative but to dismiss you as a result of the fight you have been accused of initiating. You can be assured that I will do everything possible to get to the truth of the matter. Should I find that events are as you have stated, I will make sure that you will be properly compensated. Please accept my apology, and please do not tell anyone of our conversation here today. I wish you the absolute best. You are a fine young man undeserving of the predicament you find yourself in."

Within the span of about forty minutes, the phone rang in Ms. Brooks' office and the voice at the other end of the line inquired if she had completed the job. She was well aware of what was being asked of her but questioned what job the caller was speaking of. The speaker made it clear that it was in reference to Freddie's termination when saying, "You couldn't find a way to make it happen, so I took care of it." She begrudgingly offered a job well done to the obnoxious, poor excuse of a human being, and asked how it was accomplished. No answer to the question was provided, no parting message was delivered, and the next sound was the phone being placed on the receiver.

Freddie went to say goodbye to Enzo, who was aware of his termination, and who expressed his misbelief and sorrow over the chain of events. Enzo did say he would meet him on

Saturday, same time, same place. He trudged his way home, in no hurry to deliver the bad news to his mother and father. He was full of thoughts as to what his next steps would be. He wondered, do I go in search of a job or will that be a case of futility. He could not see any good coming from that endeavor and was quite despondent over his dilemma. His need to come up with a solution pervaded his every thought. He knew Saturdays would be different now since he had no means to earn his mad money for their restaurant visits. It seemed to him that this was the most bothersome walk back home that he could imagine. *How would I help with family expenses without a regular paycheck every week?* He could not conjure up any solution and was growing weary and frustrated with his failure to do so.

His mother was at the door when he arrived and cheerfully greeted him with, "Well how is my favorite son this fine day?" There was a long period of silence before he was able to muster the courage to deliver the bad news. Due to the long break in time, Maureen suspected that all was not right with him that day. She braced herself to hear the news. He related all that had taken place and how the end result affected him. It was bad news, not to her liking, but what bothered her most, was how he kept being dealt such hurtful blows in his young life. She silently whispered to herself, "How do I find an answer to his problems?"

Conor called to inform Maureen that he would be late for dinner due to an unexpected visit from members of the Corporate Office. She questioned if he knew the reason for the visit, to which he answered, "I have no idea. You and Freddie should eat without me as I am not sure how long the meeting might last."

The rest of the week was spent wondering as to what could be coming next for the Ryan family. The time passed slowly for everyone. Freddie was already aware of his fate. Maureen was waiting for a call from the police to set up the time and place for the requested meeting. Meanwhile, Conor was in limbo, awaiting an answer from the Corporate Office. He was advised not to report for work the rest of the week until a decision was reached deciding his future. The only bright spot was that he would be paid during the time spent determining the outcome. During the visit at his office, he was advised that he had violated a company policy regarding his offering of samples. Policy dictated that the samples he gave to Balicki's father were to be supplied to doctors only. They were to be dispensed as prescriptions emanating from the various doctors having received the samples. The impending decision would ultimately decide Conor's future with the company. There was no sunshine beaming down on the family at this time. The mood was dark, and their emotions ranged from unhappiness, to worried, and overly scared. The one positive note was the fact that this was a family intent on clearing itself of any wrongdoing. Maureen was of the mindset to do whatever it would take to make things right again. She was exceptionally worried about the effect this could have on her pride and joy, Freddie.

The week passed, and still no word regarding Conor's highly anticipated decision. Maureen persisted in trying to get the meeting arranged with the police. Freddie was depressed, an emotion that never frequented him throughout his lifetime. He had no intentions of meeting with Enzo as he had done for the past several months. Tomorrow was to be a visit to the waterfront to enjoy a luncheon at one of the restaurants operating there. He would not spend his money frivolously until he was able to start earning a paycheck again. He had no intention of having his friend pay for the meal. His mind was made up. There would be no Saturday outing tomorrow.

Saturday morning was ablaze with bright sunshine and a prediction of warmer than usual temperatures. Maureen was doing everything she could to brighten the mood in the household. She was singing along with the song being played on the radio as she went about preparing breakfast for her loved ones. It brought a smile to her two men who patiently waited for the morning meal to be served. It appeared the smile was the result of Maureen's melodic voice gently filling the room. They knew it was her way of trying to shore up their spirits. The breakfast meal, the togetherness they felt, along with her singing, helped in reducing the malaise that permeated the air. Conor thanked her for breakfast and her welcome rendition of "Here Comes the Sun." It was inspiring. "I sure did like your moves to go along with the song." Maureen predicted, "Today is the first day of what will be our victory in the battle we are facing. Let's get up and start doing something about it." Freddie announced, "Mom, I am going to meet Enzo and go to the gym. I am going to get myself ready to win this fight." "Now that is more like the Freddie that I know and love." Conor chimed in saying, "I don't dare go to the gym for fear I would end up in the hospital."

CHAPTER TWELVE:

ANSWERING THE CALL TO ACTION

As Freddie was on the way to meet his faithful friend, he felt a sense of urgency and did not quite know exactly what it was all about. He met his buddy in their normal meeting place, and they were both excited to see each other. "Freddie, I am so glad to see you. I wasn't sure that you would be coming today. I am really happy that you decided to come." "To be honest I wasn't sure that I would be here today. I guess I owe it all to my mom and her infectious rendition of "Here Comes the Sun." "What is that all about?" coming from Enzo. "Oh nothing, I'll tell you later."

Minutes later they entered the domain of the illustrious B.J., who, as usual, was there to welcome them to the number one gym in Paducah. "Well champs, how am I going to be able to help you two today? You both need all the help you can get." Enzo blurted out, "I don't see anyone here capable of delivering that help, do you, Freddie?" Freddie had exited the scene and was seeking some gloves in order to take his frustrations out on a punching bag. It didn't take him long to secure what he was looking for and to get started brutally punching away at his would-be adversary. "Whoa, slow down there, champ, or you are going to hurt yourself. I am going to wrap your hands before you cause yourself a problem. What brings this action of yours about?" Freddie paused, and gave no answer to the question, had his hands wrapped and went about furiously punching away. B.J. came up to him again and asked if he could talk to him. "Let's go sit down for a bit where we don't have to hear all of the racket in here. Is that okay with you?" "Sure, where do we go?" "It may strike you as a surprise, but I do have an office in here."

They sat down in the upstairs office where Freddie was able to explain all that had happened to him this past week. B.J. was an ardent listener and absorbed all that he had to convey. The story that Freddie had to unravel was disturbing to him and caused him to pause for a prolonged period of time. "Freddie, I don't know what you aim to do about your predicament, but I want to lend a word of caution to you. You seem to be bent towards doing something you may regret. I am here to help you. I offer my help as an instructor and also as a personal friend. What you learn here can be unwisely used as a brawler, or safely as a boxer. Brawling can get you in trouble. You could possibly injure a person for life, or even cause the death of an opponent. Boxing allows you to fight in a regulated and safe manner."

B.J. continued on, "You have a problem to solve, and that is to secure employment. Your previous history had shown that trying to do so proved to be fruitless for long periods of time. Under your present circumstances, it may be impossible to be hired. Boxing can earn you money by being engaged in bouts with equally matched opponents. I once told you that I see promise in your ability to engage in the sport. You have been gifted with qualities that I see in you, allowing for you to become a worthy contender. I can, and I will train you to be the best you can be. It's your decision to make. I am offering you what I believe to be an answer to your immediate problem. I hope that whatever decision you make regarding becoming a boxer is given careful consideration by you. I wish the best to you no matter which route you choose to take."

Freddie thanked B.J. and returned to his previous activity. He once again started to expend his energy by visiting repeated blows to the punching bag he was punishing before their little meeting. All the while he was hammering away, his mind was engaged in the process of sorting out what he had been told. His thoughts centered around the fact that he did not enjoy fighting. They were flitting back and forth between several different concerns. It was a known fact that future employment would be hard to find, and there was an immediate need to be met. They then shifted and centered on the need for cash in order to help support the family. He wondered if he could possibly engage in something that he had no desire for.

Enzo was preoccupied with completing his regimen which would require another thirty minutes or so. His mind was crammed with thoughts of something good to eat for lunch. He hadn't any idea of what his buddy had been grappling with from the time he entered the gym. Enzo wrapped up the day's routine and was anxious to get down to the riverfront. He shouted out, "Hey B.J., where is the champ at?" "He is sitting here with me figuring out all the money he is going to earn in his new endeavor. Come join us."

They departed hearing a late shoutout from B.J., "I will see you here Monday morning at eight. Don't be late." Enzo smirked and sarcastically replied, "Don't worry *Edgar Alan*, he will be there." He turned to Freddie, chuckled, and said, "The guy thinks he's a poet now. Anyways, champ, it looks as if we have a lot to discuss on our way to lunch." "Enzo, I won't be able to join you. Now that I don't have a job, I can't afford to be extravagant." "Hey, I can, and I will buy your lunch. It is exactly what you would do for me if I were faced with the problem. Besides, maybe B.J. doesn't want you to be eating too much. That will save me money. Start talking, what's going on?"

As they walked on, Freddie said, "Let me begin by telling you it is beginning to be an overly complex situation. You are already aware of the fact that I do not have a job. The skinny is that my dad has been placed on probationary leave during which he is still being paid. His employer is in the process of determining whether he is subject to losing his job due to an infraction of company policy. I am not at liberty today to relate what the offense might have been. I am almost sure that he will lose his job until the air is cleared. If that were to happen, I will have to become the sole supporter of our family. Right now, I am incapable of providing one red cent to help defray expenses."

"Now, to give you the rest of the story. I had a difficult decision to make and said yes only because of what I just told you. In order to pick up some cash, I have decided to get involved in the boxing game. B.J. tells me that I exhibit signs of having the tools needed to make it in the sport. I don't know that I do. Time will tell if that is a fact or not. I do know that I do not have the stomach for injuring another human being. That is one big hurdle that I will have to surmount if I am to end up in the ring."

As Freddie continued to converse with his pal, Maureen was on the phone talking to the Desk Seargent at the Police Station. It had been agreed that they would meet at the designated location she had chosen. The police would arrive in a Plain Wrapper in order not to draw any attention. She was advised that there was one stipulation she should be aware of. Should the detectives conclude that conditions exist suggesting duplicity on his part, he will be taken into custody. She stated that she was confident the eventuality of that being the case was remote. "Alright then, Ma'am. We will see you at 7:30 p.m., Thursday. It would be better for you to arrive earlier than the time given. For the sake of caution, I suggest you, your husband, and son make a stop at the grocery store, or wherever you choose, and then take an indirect route to your destination. There will be an unidentifiable plainclothes policeman in attendance before you are to arrive. He may appear rough looking and possibly cause you some consternation. To allay your fears, he will be wearing a dark blue stocking cap with two bands of white striping. It is not customized department apparel. He ended his call by questioning her if she understood the details and asked if she had any questions.

Two loyal friends continued to converse as they were on their last twenty minutes of the long walk. Freddie filled Enzo in on every aspect of past and present happenings and advised him that he would be made aware of any future plans. Enzo told the champ that he would take care of the little weasel, Toby, for what he did to him. Freddie exclaimed, "Enzo, do not do anything. I need for you to be our eyes and ears at the store. I don't want you to be terminated for fighting. I would appreciate you informing me of any suspicious activity you might observe. The message was received loud and clear, and Enzo told him he could count on him. They arrived at their chosen eating establishment just as a large group was exiting the restaurant. Enzo remarked, "Great, that should mean there will be a lot of empty tables. Let's get in there and sink our teeth into some fine food."

As soon as they were seated, a waiter arrived and greeted them. They both ordered waters, which was promptly brought to them. They placed their food order, and while they were waiting, started a discussion regarding the interior. Both of them were quite impressed with the cleanliness and the furnishings. It was bright and well-lit and did not offer blaring music or other interrupting sounds. They agreed that the right decision was made regarding their selection. The important test was to come, that being the taste of the food. Freddie instructed Enzo not to look over to a big corner booth. It appeared the patrons there bore some similarities to the large group who left as they entered. They were all young, dressed in a casual manner, and uncharacteristically toted bags and cases of all different sorts. After taking a brief glance over toward their location, Enzo whispered, "They sure don't appear to be the All-American type either." Quietly Freddie in a hushed voice alerted him, "No, and what is more troubling is that I recognize the big guy as being pictured in a recent photo my mom secured. I will fill you in after we leave. Our food is coming our way now."

The two sleuths finish their expertly prepared food and concur that the place passed all of the tests. Freddie said, "All but one. That being the clientele. I guess we can't judge the place poorly for something out of their control, can we?"

The conversation continued outside, and fortunately the subject about the photo was never rehashed. Freddie was delighted that it was forgotten for now. He knew he made a mistake when he brought it up. He realized he was further jeopardizing his family, as well as the Suskind family. He felt that it could put Enzo in jeopardy also. He knew better than to refer to the man in the picture because it would surely turn the spotlight on the photo.

CHAPTER THIRTEEN:
THE WINDS OF TIME BEGIN TO BLOW

The conversation early in the week centered around what was going to be disclosed to the police. It was Maureen's feeling that nothing should be held back. Her direction was, "stick to the truth, and answer all questions that are asked of you. It is easy to recollect the answer to rephrased questions when all you have to do is stick to the truth. Do not, under any circumstance, admit to being guilty of any wrongdoing other than what you submitted. Your first supply was done because of the threat that was made to you. Subsequent dispensements were also made under duress, and were either delayed by you, or were short of the requested amount. You are now receiving threats to the family because you are balking on deliveries. It should become evident to the investigators that you were an unwilling accomplice, are now seeking protection because you do not want to continue supplying the drug dealer. The fact you do not currently have access to drugs due to your forced layoff complicates matters all the more."

Conor replied, "I am in total agreement that all you have stated is fact, good advice, and is consistent with what my responses will be. I am worried that I might say something that will be misinterpreted by them and will be accused of something I did not do." "Telling the truth, and not dodging

any of the questions asked of you will help prevent that
eventuality."

Freddie's week had been extremely hectic. The chatter about
Thursday's proposed meeting, coupled with all the advice
thrown at him by B.J. had him rattled. B.J. was being
forthright with him, advising him of possible pitfalls, and
cautioning him to be patient. "Champ, I--" Freddie
interrupted him and pleaded with him not to refer to him as
"champ." "I am going to find it hard to honor your request,
but I will earnestly try not to do so. What I wanted to convey
to you was that this process will take time. I do not intend to
throw you into the ring until I am satisfied you are
professionally trained. I want to be sure you are prepared to
protect yourself, and to carry the fight to your opponent.
Your first several fights will be with opponents I choose.
They won't be pushovers; they will be fighters that will stand
in there and demand you be aware of their ability to put a
hurt on you. Doing so will allow me to determine your
readiness, and to see if you have heart for the game.

As the week wound down, the Ryan household was full of
anticipation and concern. Conor asked Maureen, "What if
they don't believe me? They might take me into custody."
Maureen replied, "Worrying about what might be is a waste
of energy and deprives you of precious time to effectively
plan on what to do. There is an old saying, 'You Cannot
Control the Wind, but You Can Adjust Your Sail.' The
situation you find yourself in is beyond your control. What
you can control is how you respond and react to it. Be

honest, have faith, and remember that Freddie and I believe in you and are vouching for you. You needn't worry about a thing."

Wednesday morning found Freddie at the gym once again, listening to sage advice and absorbing instructions from his newly acquired fight manager/trainer. "You will be engaged in a regimen that calls for strict adherence to the plan. It is an uphill battle and requires diligence and fortitude on your part. You are going to go through an experience much like the metamorphosis an insect goes through while changing from egg to adulthood. You are going to be transformed from a potential fighter to a polished professional boxer. What it is going to take is your willingness to make it happen. How long it will take depends on how badly you want it. Now, I suggest we make this the first day of training. Get ready for punishment and pain, and always remember you were made aware of what to expect."

As Freddie left the gym, he was visited by aching muscles, some of which he didn't know he had, or know could hurt so much. He knew now what B.J. warned him of was spoken truth. It was going to be a tough grind. He was sure of one thing. He may not want this, but he needed it. He had to earn cash. He had to be of help to his parents when they were so badly in need of help.

Arriving home he was made aware of the dread that his father was experiencing, and it bothered him to see it. After dinner they gathered in the small, cramped living room and discussed what they thought were defensive moves on their part. Not knowing what to expect was the worst part of their ordeal. Maureen bolstered Conor by saying, "Your willingness to cooperate, along with the pictures we have, are going to put you in a positive light right from the beginning. They are going to be grateful that you supplied the photos to them. I am sure that having those as evidence will do much to corroborate your testimony and aid them in breaking up the drug ring. Let's all get to bed so we will be well rested for whatever tomorrow may bring." Freddie blurted out, "Amen, I am ready."

Thursday morning found Freddie moving at a slower than usual pace getting ready to depart for the house of pain. He wondered if an intelligent person would be subjecting himself to more of the same. He walked into the gym, and was asked by B.J., "Freddie, what doesn't hurt you today?" "I believe you already know that the answer is nothing. My hair even hurts me. My stomach sure does." "Your hair? Your stomach is to be expected and is the reason we are going to concentrate on strengthening your core muscles. I am going to change the muscles you have so that your abdomen and back muscles are going to become a protective shield. I want your abdomen to become a plate of steel, and your back muscles to aid you in improving your balance needed to effectively move while avoiding blows. We need the back muscles to be strengthened in order to start some heavy lifting. Your whole body is in for a transformation. All for the good. All meant to enable you to absorb punches you are unable to deflect. Time to get to work."

He returned home from the gym and wondered if he would be able to attend tonight's meeting. He was hurting worse than he was yesterday. As strong as he felt about not going, he knew he had no choice but to go. He was going to be there if his dad needed his support. Maureen was ready for whatever the night was to bring. She was fortified by her faith knowing that it was strong, and that right would prevail.

They followed the route prescribed for them and arrived at what was the residence of a friend of a retired patrolman from the Paducah Police Department. Every precaution was taken to ensure that in the event they were followed, the meeting place did not indicate the potential for police presence. It appeared from all indications that nobody attempted to follow them. They were relieved about how smooth that seemed to be accomplished and entered the house. The first thing they noticed was a raggedy bearded man. He was wearing a blue stocking cap with two bands of white striping covering what was most likely a frosted curly fake toupee. He appeared just as they were told. He made no attempt to strike up a conversation and sat quietly observing their arrival. In short order, two Brown Wrappers pulled up within minutes of each other. The occupants exited their vehicles and entered separately, and upon entering identified themselves as members of the vice squad that was working the case. After seeing the credentials and badges of the officers a feeling of ease was starting to settle in with the Ryan family.

A tall husky looking young man, who appeared to be the lead investigator invited them to take a seat. No time was wasted in pointing out that the raggedy gentleman was an undercover plainclothes officer working on the case. Freddie had been eyeing him as soon as they entered the premises. There was something about this man that piqued his interest. Freddie continued to focus on him and had a strong feeling as to who he was. Cole Hunter, the lead investigator, prompted Conor to offer whatever information he had for them. Conor presented the information just as Maureen decided for him to do. He acknowledged he was coerced into relenting to supply the first of the sample pills and continued to reluctantly provide more under increased pressure. He acknowledged to missing drops that were requested of him, and of supplying less than the requested amounts. He was fearful for the well-being of his wife and son and did not know how to respond otherwise. He was the victim of circumstances beyond his control. He explained that he finally came to realize that his only course of action was to go to the police.

The fear and anxiety that Conor was feeling about what the outcome of this meeting would bring was rapidly dissipating. He now felt confident that all would end well for him. That feeling expanded when he presented Agent Hunter with the photos of the incident at the pool parlor. He was asked how he came by the pictures and recited they were given to him by concerned citizens. "They are a family of four, were total strangers to us, and we now fear for their safety."

"Before going any further, I want you to know that we have been shadowing you for some time now. We have been on your trail ever since we came into possession of the pill bottles bearing the Amber label. We still are not aware of who it was that sent them to us. It came along with information that drugs were being supplied by a source from within the company. You probably have already picked up on the fact that your son has been under surveillance by Agent Bruce Cannon. What we learned from those activities is that your implication in this matter was a result of coercion. We are confident that both of you are willing to help us in any way you can."

"Okay, here is what I want of you. I want you to keep in contact with whoever that is. I want you to profess that you have been fired from your job, are angry because of it, and in need of a job. I will take care of making sure that you are a suspect we are trying to capture. Your employers, who we have already been in touch with, are working with us as we speak. Your job status with them is secured as long as we are confident that you have been on the up and up with us. We expect full cooperation from you in helping us break open this case. It might comfort you to know that Amber Pharmaceuticals has informed us that you have been a loyal employee. Once proven innocent of any charges, they are granting full backpay for all missed work. They further stated that you are not of the type to get involved in criminal activity. One additional bit of information is that they have been considering granting a promotion to you. They think so highly of you that they are going to try to hold off on filling the position of General Manager of the Eastern Seaboard. That possibility would probably hinge on how quickly we are able to wrap this up. We are in hopes that you continue to work with us and that we can close the case in a short period of time. I want you to know it will not be easy to do. You also should be aware that it depends totally on your full cooperation. Should you decide to work with us we will offer some financial help to keep you afloat. It will by no means be equivalent to your current pay amount. Lastly, you will be in danger all the while we are trying to get to the kingpin. What say you?"

"I may be jumping from the frying pan into the fire, but I want you to know I am at your disposal."

As they prepared to depart, Freddie looked over at the raggedy old gent and inquired if he could ask a question. Cole submitted and invited him to do so. "You may not want to reveal the identity of your agent, but I believe I know exactly who he is. Can I share that identity with you?" "Have at it, who do you think it might be?" "My observations tell me it is Bruce Cannon." "What brings you to that conclusion, son?" "It is his piercing blue eyes I noticed when visiting with him on several occasions. The real giveaway for me is his crooked index finger on his left hand, and the funny shape of the fingernail. I don't see how this might be a coincidence, and I am positive I made a correct identification." Cole smiled, and admitted, "I am sorry to have to admit you are absolutely correct. It appears that we have not covered all our bases in trying to conceal his identity. Bruce has been working with us on the case, and he has informed us that he has great respect for your integrity. He also is of the opinion that you had been wrongly fired because of trumped-up charges being lodged against you. I want you to call me Monday morning. Here is my card. Call me at the phone number listed."

Monday morning arrived and as he was requested to do, Freddie placed a call to Agent Hunter. He was greeted with, "Good morning, Freddie, how are you today? I am glad you accepted my invitation to call. Are you interested and of the mind to help me?" "How am I able to help you?" "I want to put you in as a cashier at the new store being opened by the owner of the store you were working at. Our sources inform us that the acquisition was held up due to a shortage of cash on Mr. Swanson's part. It appears the seller agreed to a price that Swanson was able to afford. The sale had stalled because he did not want to have to borrow any funds in order to buy the store." "They won't hire me. I have been fired from his store in Paducah." "They will hire Mike Sloan, a newcomer to the area. You are to become Mike Sloan. That will be your new identity." "And how does that happen?" "Our source we use to change identities will take care of that matter. He is good at what he does." "Is he better than the source you used to transform Bruce Cannon?" "Actually, it is one and the same. This time I will be more demanding of his makeover. I was at fault in approving Cannon's identity change. That is what happens when the bad guys start outpacing you. When he is done with you, even your own mother won't be able to recognize you. I give you my complete assurance in the matter. I can assure you a small stipend will be paid to you, in addition to all of your living expenses being covered while you are serving us. You will be separated from your family. You will have to live in the Marion area at a Safe House we have secured. You will have no contact with anybody but me. You should be able to continue with whatever your normal off-duty routine is. We will be monitoring you while at work as well as when you are off duty. All you have to do for us is observe comings and goings of certain individuals. We will make their identities known to you. We will not put you in harm's way, and we expect you to obey our demands regarding your safety. I realize that this is not an easy decision for you to make. I cannot force you to make it. What you need to know is that with your help we can shorten the span of time it will take to bring them down. The decision lies with you. Are you with us?" "I want to say yes now, but I need a day or two to ensure I wrap up a few things. I want to be certain it does not interfere with my plans for the future." "Okay then, we will call you at 9:00 a.m. on Thursday of this week. I expect a final answer on that day. I don't want to lose time which will certainly benefit the drug dealers." "Okay, Thursday at 9:00 a.m. it is. I will be ready to give you an answer."

CHAPTER FOURTEEN:

A TIME FOR CHANGE

Tuesday morning found Freddie at the gym engaged in the prescribed routine readying him for his introduction to the fight game. His mind was preoccupied with questions. *How do I inform B.J. about my sudden disappearance without letting the cat out of the bag? How do I request details for further training routines?* He finally concluded that he had to be sneaky to achieve what was required. He knew that the training routine had to continue in a proper and measurable manner. He wanted some amateur bouts to be arranged as soon as possible upon his return. Freddie continued with his training that had been planned for him and was content on waiting until tomorrow came to break the news to B.J.

A foreboding was building in the Ryan household and a feeling of uncertainty was settling in. Conor was questioning his ability to carry out what had been requested of him. As he was deliberating the consequences of his approval to do so, a call came in from Cole. "Hello, Conor speaking." "Conor, Cole here. I felt the need to get back to you and bring you up to date on recent developments. First of all, I want you to be fully aware of the danger you are placing yourself in. As we discussed earlier, we are dealing with dangerous people who have little regard for the lives of others. You will not be trusted and may be placed in a position to prove your trust to their cause. We have become alerted to the fact that an execution has been carried out within their ranks. It seems that the top dog is dissatisfied with the lack of progress. He is known to be on a warpath of sorts. In our previous conversations, you were advised that we would have no open line of communication, nor do we have any ideas on how to set something up. You suggested that you would try to develop some sort of code entailing your hobby of birdwatching. The problem is, how do you manage to get the info to the right party? The use of a code can be dangerous if it could be easily interpreted by one of them. I can tell you this, we do have a mole in place at the new store but have been unable to place one inside of their ring. My attempts to enlist the aid of a retired agent who was good at what he did, has not been met with success. He was, without a doubt, one of the best undercover agents the agency had. If anybody could insert themselves into their organization, he could. Unfortunately, his last answer to me was, 'You can't pay me enough to touch that job.'

"My question to you now is, do you realize what you are up against, and do you still want to carry it out? I can assure you that we find no wrongdoing on your part, and you are cleared of any suspicion in the matter." Conor assured him. "I signed up for the assignment, knowing I was not guilty of any implication. I did that because I wanted to help eradicate a nemesis to society. I have not changed my mind in regard to continuing on with what I signed on to do. I am all in."

Before he terminated the call, he cautioned Cole to start at the end and proceed to the beginning of the book to decipher the message. He also told him that he would be using different colors of ink to spell out whatever he would be able to learn. "I have no idea where I will be held, no idea of where to send the book, or who I will have to deliver it."

Cole had to shoot from the hip in order to get some guiding information to Conor. This could very well be the last time they would be able to communicate together. "Here is what I am able to tell you, all of which I have to make happen. My second-in-command believes he has been able to convince our retiree to get on board with us. He is our only hope. Should we make that work, you will be able to identify him by the color of the coat he will be wearing. It will be of an amber tone. Don't go to him. He will come to you. He will have to work out the delivery dilemma. He will be made aware of the identity of the plant at the Marion store, who is to receive the book. I will have two code specialists on hand to decipher your message. Try to get an address off of some incoming flyer or envelope that might be lying around. Start that information from the beginning to the end of the book. One last piece of information. The agent's name is Axel. He will identify himself to you. I believe I have covered all that is necessary in order to make things work. Good luck to you."

When Freddie arrived at home, he found his dad and mother engaged in worried conversation, wondering when the call that would put him in harm's way would come. They greeted him and requested he sit down and join in with them. It was quite apparent to him that what had been asked of his father was of grave concern to both of them. It certainly was bothering him at the present time. His mother would shortly be faced with her husband in imminent danger, and her son absent from her life for an unknown period of time. The picture he was presently faced with intensified his need for a *"yes"* answer regarding his commitment to become involved. *The sooner I get on with my part, the sooner the end will be in sight.*

The next day Freddie was engaged in a strenuous workout. He found himself rope jumping, skipping around the ring, on a three-mile run, and then back on the speed bag for an extended period of time. The process of getting his legs in shape had begun. He enjoyed every minute of his workout and did not seem to show any signs of exhaustion in any phase of the training routine. The distance of his planned runs would slowly increase to five miles, alternating between two or three times every other week. The time had come for him to leave to return home, and he shouted out, "See you tomorrow, B.J." The information received from Cole Hunter did not make his leaving any easier. Freddie left the premises without informing B.J. of his impending departure.

Conor received another call informing him not to do anything stupid. Make sure you are there Friday, and don't go to the police and divulge any information. "You know we keep a close watch on your comings and goings." Conor retorted, "You don't need to concern yourself about that. I haven't made any attempt to go to the police. I don't intend to entrap myself. Besides, I need help from you. I will see you Friday evening."

Thursday morning found an anxious Freddie awaiting the expected 9:00 a.m. telephone call. At precisely that time, the call came in just as it had been planned. "Good morning, Freddie speaking." "And a good morning to you also. Do you have an answer for me this fine day?" "I sure do. I am ready to do whatever it is you might ask of me. Give me the word on what I need to do next." "What I would like is for you to meet me this evening at 629 Husband Road at 7:30 p.m. That is the home of our makeover specialist. A ride has been arranged for you. Proceed to go east for two blocks from your residence. At the corner you will see a dark blue truck with a bumper sticker with the American flag displayed on it. Your driver will identify himself as Mickey Mouse. The makeover artist will take some pictures and ask a few questions to help in determining what he needs to get the results we want. It should not require more than an hour of your time. You and I will have no further contact until you are to assume the identity of Mike Sloan. I have all of the paperwork and credentials you will need while you're masquerading as Sloan and walking in his shoes. They will be given to you by a female agent at the Safe House where you will be residing. She will be masquerading as the real estate agent. The cupboard and the refrigerator will be well stocked before you arrive. She will furnish you pictures as well as pertinent information regarding the bozos we want you to be on the lookout for. Monday morning, your transformation will take place. You will be driven to where you are to report for the makeover. You are to be fully prepared to go directly to Marion once that is completed. You tell your mother and father that you are going for training with the National Guard. Paperwork confirming your training location, time of departure, and mode of transportation will be noted in that correspondence. The packet was mailed out in Wednesday's noon mail. You are to advise them that this is necessary in order to earn ready cash. You had no choice as to the departure date. You accepted this date rather than wait for next month's boot camp. You will have no further contact with your parents after Sunday since communication is not allowed at boot camp. Any questions so far?" "No, sir."

"You have a 2:00 PM interview appointment on Monday at the Supermarket. That has all been arranged. Be sure to be on time. The store is three blocks distant from your living quarters. On the kitchen table will be a special edition flyer from the store. There is a little directional map, including the address, in the bottom left corner of the first page. It should not take you more than fifteen minutes to reach the store. I will be in touch with you at 4:30 p.m. I will have additional instructions for you once you get settled in. By the way, an army vehicle will be picking you up at 4:00 a.m., Monday morning. Enjoy your day."

Freddie was delighted that he had bona fide information to give to B.J. and to Enzo. The fake paperwork should answer all the questions and satisfy the reason for his absence. His emotions were about to get the best of him. Leaving his parents, his friend, and missing the next stages of his training caused him despair. His utmost wish was that the absence would not be for long.

The day passed fast for Freddie while it seemed like an eternity to Maureen and Conor, who had yet to hear when he would become a part of smashing the drug ring. Conor did receive one call which requested his presence at the pool hall Friday evening. It was not something he was looking forward to but there was a certain sense of security in the fact that Maureen knew exactly where he would be and who he would be with.

The Ryan household was a beehive of activity from the time they had arisen. Freddie was readying himself for what might be his last visit to the gym in a while. He unconsciously said, "Is it possible it will be my last?" Maureen, who just exited her bedroom, heard his muttering, and asked, "Did you say something to me?" "Oh, no mom. I guess I was just babbling. It is getting to be a habit." "Well, shake it up because the casserole I made for this morning's breakfast is about to come out of the oven." "You won't have to call me twice. I love it when you make that. It's like a Smorgasbord to me." They were all at the table awaiting the buzzer on the oven to ring signaling the masterpiece was ready. Maureen, in her attempt to pick up the hot dish tilted it and some of the hot liquid came spilling over the edge and poured out over her hand. Her immediate reaction was to rinse her hand under cold running water. Conor filled a large bowl with ice cubes and had her submerge her hand into the ice filled bowl. The interruption delayed breakfast for an appreciable amount of time. What should have been an enjoyable treat lost most of its appeal. Maureen's hand did not engender an overly amount of concern. It was decided that a doctor's visit did not appear to be necessary. Conor advised her to take all necessary precautions in order not to aggravate the burn area. She needed to concentrate on healing and pay close attention to signs of infection. They did not want for complications to set in.

CHAPTER FIFTEEN:

PUTTING THE PIECES IN PLACE

It was dizzying for Freddie who was trying to focus on his instructions from Head Agent Cole Hunter while coping with all of his other concerns. It would not be easy leaving his father, who would be placed in the path of danger, and his mother, especially now with her burnt hand. Then there was his regret of leaving Enzo, and his now manager B.J. There was sufficient reason for concern of his own safety which did not seem to be one of the bothersome thoughts he was wrestling with. He felt quite capable of handling whatever would present itself to him. He made a commitment to aid in breaking up a drug ring and he wanted to get on with the show. His greatest motivation to do so was greatly influenced over his apprehension for his father's safety.

While on the way to what had become a go-to place for him, he reflected on being away from his mother, who would be left alone and vulnerable if something should go wrong. He realized these were not rational people that he and his father would be dealing with. A light bulb lit up in his mind and he realized that he had Enzo to rely on if the need arose. He was overcome with gratitude for the friendship that had been forged between them. He hoped that he might be able to go to the gym on Saturday and see both Enzo and B.J. before he left.

When he arrived at the gym, he was surprised to see an ambulance parked out in front of the entrance. Thankfully, it was not there to treat B.J., who had been having some health issues lately. He did find his manager shaken up as a result of the activity going on inside. One of the sparring partners who suffered a devastating blow to his nose was hemorrhaging and required medical attention. The EMT's had finished administering to him and were packing up to leave as he entered the building. All was under control and the victim was through for the day. He probably would be sporting packing gauze in his nostril for a few days. If that was not an answer to his need, the medic told him he would need to see a doctor to have cautery performed in order to seal the blood vessels.

It was time for him to engage in today's training routine. He wanted to leave ample time to talk to B.J. in case he would not be able to return on Saturday. It was his desire to be able to return so he could enlist Enzo's aid if it was needed. He also wanted the opportunity to personally inform him of the reason for his sudden departure. His training exercises for the day were a healthy dose of medicine to him. It was welcome relief from all of the thoughts that were previously bouncing around in his mind. What he wanted now was the words needed to accomplish what had to be conveyed to his knowledgeable manager.

Freddie ambled over to the office where B.J. sought solitude from the hustle and bustle that was omnipresent in the muscle building structure that housed the best gym in Paducah, Kentucky. He found B.J. sitting and enjoying the serenity the office provided to him. Freddie engaged him in small talk to soften the effect his departure news may have on him. In spite of his reluctance to do so, the time had arrived to make it happen. He filled B.J. in on all of the pertinent information that was required of him. He was greeted with, "Why so sudden and so secretive?" to which he replied, "Current circumstances leave me no choice. You can be assured of the fact that I will be back as soon as my National Guard training is completed. I would appreciate it if you could set up a training regimen for me. I don't want to lose a skip in the beat while being away. Is it possible for you to do that for me?" "I can, but you are going to have to guard against over exercising, considering you will be engaged in their physical training requirements. Will you be here tomorrow?" "It is my hope to be. It is in my plans to be here unless something unexpected should surface." "Okay, I will draw something up this evening. You need to give me a way to get them to you should you not be here tomorrow. I will say goodbye and extend my wishes for good luck to you should that become the case." They exchanged greetings and a hug and departed with nothing further being spoken. It was a sad moment for both of them.

On the way home, he was visited again with thoughts regarding his upcoming venture. He migrated from those to the sad thoughts resulting from the meeting he had just experienced. On his arrival, he was presented with a good news, bad news situation. The good news being that Conor had been contacted, the bad news that he was he might be expected to begin his involvement as soon as his meeting tonight dictated. Both of them would be taken out of Maureen's life almost simultaneously. Instructions were laid out for Conor; a contact person had been named and means for him to hopefully make contact were discussed. Tonight, his objective was to convince the party he was meeting that he needed employment with them due to being fired. He also sought protection from the police. They were in search of him now. The police had wrecked his life. He had no plans to return home for fear they would be awaiting his return. He needed their help. It was a wonder to him that he had not been picked up by the police by now. He had to become one of them.

They were seated for what would be the last meal together for an extended time. Conor had flashes of guilt. He thought about how if he had refused the elder Balicki's first request and reported it to the police, things would be different now. There were now three people under threat of violence, when it should have been only him. He was astute enough to realize reflecting on the past only muddles the mind. There was time for only clear thinking from this point on. He was gratified by the fact that Maureen would be afforded round-the-clock protection until the incident was wrapped up. He found no solace in the fact that Freddie would not be with her until his supposed National Guard training was completed.

A hurried meal was in order so that Conor would arrive in a timely manner and not give cause for them to be suspect of his actions. After finishing the meal, he went about preparing a travel bag with necessary toiletries. He packed lightly, adding clean underclothes, should they expect his services to begin immediately. He felt they would, allowing them to have him under their control where his every move could be monitored. An after thought prodded him to pack his cherished album that identifies the different species of birds.

"Goodbye," and "God be with you," were passed to him by both of his admirers. He wanted a quick departure to avoid sentimental feelings from spilling over before he could make his exit. "Goodbye to both of you. I will be back when this sticky mess comes to an end. I love you both dearly. Please be mindful of your safety. God bless and keep you." As he walked out the door, Freddie lamented, saying to his mother, "If I had only listened to you and ran away from that fight with Balicki, we wouldn't be in this quagmire we find ourselves in."

Maureen, who was emotionally drained, mustered the strength to reply, "Freddie dear, you had no control over that incident. Don't beat yourself up over it. We need to save our strength so we can handle whatever else is to beset us. Keep the faith, we will overcome our difficulties." About three long hours after Conor had left for his demanded meeting, the telephone rang. It rang once, then stopped. It rang twice a second time, then stopped. The first was confirmation from Conor signaling all was well. The second signaled he had been requested to stay on. Maureen and Freddie felt good about the "all is well" message but had reservations about the role he had assumed. His contact yelled at him, "What are you doing? Get off that phone." "I was trying to call my wife." "I was told there were to be no calls made by you. My orders were to take you to where we are now going." Conor felt good about the fact that they had set up some ways to communicate in case he had no use of a phone. Thankfully, he had completed one of the means to signal he was fine before that was to happen.

They had both settled in and were about ready to call it a night when another call came in. Freddie anticipated it to be a call from Cole, necessitating his urgent need for some service to be fulfilled. It was not. The caller, who he was happy was calling, was none other than Enzo. It was a pleasant surprise. "Enzo how are you? I am so glad you called. You will be at the gym tomorrow, won't you?" "Oh yes, what I am calling you about now is to find out if you had received a call from Ms. Black. It seems that Toby has admitted that the supposed confrontation you were to have had with him was a set up. I couldn't wait until tomorrow to inform you of the fact. He confessed that he was forced into pulling off the stunt by a fellow department employee. I do not know who that was. All the news I have been privy to indicated that everybody was excited to hear the truth. They all are happy to hear that you did not do anything and had been falsely accused. I am so glad that Toby was able to admit his part in the wrongdoing but what I am most happy about is that I did nothing to harm Toby, thanks to your advice. I knew the truth would surface sooner or later. Thankfully, it was sooner. I'll see you tomorrow, good night now." "Good night to you, and thanks for informing me of the welcome news. I have a lot to tell you tomorrow, and I have a special favor to ask of you. I know what you are thinking. No, it has to wait until tomorrow." Enzo let out a "Dang it," and abruptly hung up.

CHAPTER SIXTEEN:

GOODBYES ARE HARD TO SAY

It appeared to Freddie like somebody had pressed the full steam ahead button. Activity had gone from a hurry up and wait situation to running at full throttle. He knew he had a few matters yet to complete and figured he had better give them his full attention. It would require an early to bed evening and an early to rise morning. The need to do so was a distasteful proposition in view of the fact that this was the last weekend he would be spending with his mother for some time. Maureen, whose air had been sucked out of her, was in dire need of rest. She was reluctant to inform Freddie of the fact and felt she needed to tough it out. Fortunately for both of them, she relinquished and excused herself for having to retire so early. He was pleased that she made the decision to turn in because he could see she was sorely in need of some recuperative sleep. He felt remorseful at the same time, but knew the decision was in the best interest of the family. "Mom, you sleep in tomorrow. I am going to rise early, and I will prepare my own breakfast. You need all the rest you can get. I will finish what I need to do, and I will return home early. I have a yearning for calves liver and onions. If that suits you, I will stop at the market and pick some up." "That suits me just fine.

It's funny, but I have had a yearning for some myself. What a coincidence. I am really going to enjoy that treat. Looking forward to your early return. Be careful. Good night now." "Good night to you also. Make sure you keep the doors locked and keep me informed as to what's going on with you tomorrow."

He was off for what would prove to be a bittersweet day for him. It would be the last enjoyable Saturday for a longer time than what he would like it to be. He was out of the apartment quick as a flash, full of excitement and concern. His buddy was waiting for him at their designated meeting place. Enzo was anxious for the information he was told he had to wait until today to hear. As soon as he spotted Freddie, his mind focused on the question he was to ask. Once he was close enough for Freddie to hear him, he blurted out, "Okay, what is the favor, and what is the information you need to tell me?" "Whoa, you need to slow down and take a deep breath. I haven't even had the chance to say good morning."

Conor was having a problem convincing his contact that he was not involved with the police. Juan, the contact, was in no mood for games and made him aware of the fact. "If you are in any way involved with the police, your life and that of your wife and son are not worth two cents. We don't play games. You better be listening to what I am telling you. You are going to have to earn our trust. I will tell you right now, I don't trust you at all. As for us supplying you with a job, that is a joke. We don't owe you anything. You owe us and are going to have to do something to make it up to us. Do you understand what I am saying to you?" "Yes, I told you I am running from the police, what makes you think that I am foolish enough to put myself at risk?"

"Enzo, when we arrive at the gym, I would like to go through my training routine first and get together with B.J. before I clue you in on what's going on. I will also tell you what the favor is that I would like from you. Bear with me for just a bit longer."

It took him no time at all to get involved with his routine, which he did with gusto. He needed to make the most of this, his last opportunity to have availability to all the training equipment. It was his hope that while away he would be able to maintain his present fitness condition. He knew he was not going to be able to improve it at all. There was no desire on his part to start from the beginning again. He was in a hurry to make a few dollars in order to keep his mother afloat. There was rent and utilities that had to be paid, and what little savings were available would not last long. He was sure that the money promised him from Cole would not be available for long after their mission was successfully completed. His thoughts turned to a discussion the family had had several weeks ago. After hearing a sermon at church, they wondered as a family what they could do to help the less fortunate. Now it appeared they were the ones who were in need of help.

With all that was racing around in his mind, it was difficult to concentrate on his assigned exercise routine. His body was willing, but his mind was not cooperating. It soon became apparent to him that he needed to focus in order to get the most out of his workout. Try as he may, the unwanted thoughts were winning the battle. He decided that it was time to wrap it up and sit down with B.J. in order to get the exercise package he had put together for him. He wondered if he would even be able to perform them considering what he experienced today.

B.J. was waiting anxiously for Freddie's to stop by so he could provide him with sound advice concerning his training routine. He was concerned that Freddie may overdo it and cause himself some harm. When he arrived, they wasted no time getting right down to the matter at hand. Freddie was given all the cautionary information that B.J. had to offer. The routine was meant to be a regimen that would help Freddie to maintain the level of fitness he had achieved. He had considered what type of exercises Freddie would be put through while engaged in the National Guard training program. What he was recommending would be sufficient and not cause harm. Freddie thanked B.J. for his help and for his concern in the matter and assured him that he would follow his advice to the letter. B.J. replied, "I know you will, and I want you to know that you will be on my mind. I am going to miss you. Please take care of yourself and keep in touch if you have time to do so."

Enzo came bounding in and joined in with the conversation the two were enjoying after they had taken care of business. "So, Enzo, it appears that I will just have you to contend with for a while." "And just exactly what is that supposed to mean? Have I been left out of the loop? Tell me, what's going on?" Freddie was upset that he had not informed B.J. not to bring up the subject to Enzo. He was saving that matter to be discussed before they parted. "Enzo, I had no intentions of withholding anything that I wanted you to know. I intended to tell you myself. Let's get on our way so we can talk. B.J., thanks again for everything. I will be back soon. You are a true friend." They parted on a sad note and B.J. was visibly upset about Freddie's leaving for Boot Camp.

The two buddies left to enjoy the rest of the day together. Freddie inquired of Enzo, "Would you like to go to spend the afternoon at Putt & Partake? We can have a hotdog and a soft drink for lunch. It will give us more time to discuss things." "That sounds good to me. I am all in for that." While playing, Freddie explained his need to join the National Guard to earn some much-needed cash. "You know of my dad losing his job, and of my loss of employment. It leaves us in a very bad state of affairs presently. Once I complete my training, I intend to get really serious about getting into the boxing game. That will afford me the opportunity to make some money. Should I find that not being a reality, I intend to join the Army. I will never be able to find employment around here unless somebody like Ms. Brooks clears the way for me." "I have some good news for you. Now that Toby has disclosed that you did not initiate the supposed fight, she has started to secure back pay retroactive to the date of your expulsion. He informed her as to how he was pressured into performing the stunt. I will let her know about your joining the National Guard. She said she tried calling your dad but did not get an answer to her calls. She said his work number was the only one listed as a contact in case of emergency. I was to deliver this information to you and get back to her as soon as I could."

They got their putters and balls and were next up to get on the putting course. About halfway through the game, Enzo admitted, "It's a good thing nobody can see how bad we are at this game. I'm ready for it to be over and grab a hotdog. I'm famished. How about you?" "I think we should finish the game. We might find ourselves getting better at it." "Okay with me, but let's hurry."

They turned in the equipment and headed over to the little refreshment stand. They could smell the aroma of the hot dogs cooking on the rotisserie. "Well, what are we waiting for? Let's get down to business and get our orders placed before somebody else gets in line before us." Enzo chuckled and questioned, "Now, who would that likely be since we are the only two in sight?" "You know what I mean, I'm hungry."

The order was placed, and they sat down at a table set away from the others. In a flash, a young man brought them their food order and they dug in without another word being spoken. Enzo immediately grabbed the check as soon as their waiter placed it on the table. He echoed Freddie's sentiments about their being something inviting about eating hot dogs in an outdoor setting. The fact that they were perfectly cooked and so delicious added to the allure.

Having eaten and finding themselves totally satisfied with their fare, they promptly engaged in the conversation Enzo was impatiently waiting to hear. Freddie admitted that he was going to sorely miss Enzo, and the camaraderie that he enjoyed when being together. He also shared his concern about his mother's well-being while away from her. "She will be all alone and vulnerable. I would appreciate it if you would look in on her from time to time and also stay in touch with her by phone. If it is not too much trouble, would you call her in the morning as well as in the evening before retiring for the night?" "Rest assured, I will do everything within my power to provide for her safety and well-being while you are away. I will make it a point to talk with her sometime after church on Sunday. She can inform me what I need to do to assure her that I will be there for her. I want her to be comfortable with me and not be afraid to call me at any time she may feel the need. That's what friends do for friends. You can count on me."

CHAPTER SEVENTEEN:

SETTING THE HOOK

Conor had been placed in an inner room of the house the drug runners were occupying and was not involved in any of the conversations that took place. He was still not allowed use of a phone for the purpose of calling Maureen, which troubled him considerably. He had to be allowed to let her know that he was safe at this time. Presently, he was trying to figure out a way that he could listen in on their telephone conversations. While he was concentrating on solving his dilemma, one of the two that were left behind entered his room. "You better muscle up because we have some goods coming in and we will need you to unload the truck. Wow, it is hot and stuffy in here. You can come and sit here for a bit until the truck arrives." "Would you open the transom above the door so I can get some of this fresh air into my room?" "Yeah, open it, you're a big boy. Do it yourself." "While I am sitting here, can I get my bird book? I hear a lot of chirping going on outside." "Did you bring your favorite doll along with you? You can get it also."

Time passed while Conor was engaged in looking out of the picture window in the room. He was fortunate to have several species flitting around a big Magnolia tree fairly close to the house. He inquired, "You don't happen to have some binoculars handy, do you?" "Hey Bird Man, do we look like nature lovers to you? Maybe we can snare a couple, and you can have them for lunch."

The driver pulled the large van up to the side door of the house and Conor was called to proceed with the unloading task. The undertaking took up a good part of the late afternoon and exhausted Conor appreciably. He was in no means fit for that kind of labor. As soon as he had completed the assignment, they told him to sit because his meal was ready. He was not feeling well and fidgeted with his food. "Come on muscles, finish up. We have got work to do." As soon as he finished what little he felt comfortable eating, he was told to go back to his room.

Remembering that the transom was open, he entered very quietly so that they did not detect any sounds coming from his room. The open transom might allow for him to pick up on their conversations and possibly on their end of telephone conversations. There was a call that came in about two hours after he had returned to his room. The person who answered the phone spoke in subdued tones, making it impossible to piece the conversation together. Conor found it to be very disappointing and concluded that it was of no help to have opened the transom. He was straining his mind trying to figure out what he might be able to do in order to hear better. He found that he could hear better out of his right ear, and if he sat in a certain spot, it improved his ability to pick up more of the conversation. He further found that by putting a pillow on the register, it dampened the vibration thereby eliminating competing sound. It was not long before the effect of today's strenuous activity and his constant searching for solutions found him too tired to stay awake.

Parting was not easy for either Freddie or Enzo. "We will talk tomorrow when I call to speak to your mother. Have a good night's sleep and enjoy your time with her." "Thanks again, we will be waiting for your call."

Freddie and his mother arose early Sunday morning, enjoyed breakfast together and joined the neighbors who they rode along with to go to church. Freddie's mind was elsewhere but at the church service he attended. He was focused on his concern for his mother and father, and wondered how events would play out for him in the role he was soon to assume. He became alert again when Reverend Turner related that in Psalm 23, 'the Lord protects his Sheep and fills their days with His blessings.' That message from his pastor could not have come at a timelier moment. He was suddenly infused with a feeling of hope and inner strength. He knew that all was going to end well for everybody concerned.

Time passed swiftly that Sunday. It was passing much faster than Freddie would have liked. This would be their last day together for who knows how long. There was not much that he could say to further alert his mother, or to offer her comfort. The call came in from Enzo, which seemed to provide Maureen with a calming effect. Before she handed the phone off to her son, she thanked him profusely and acknowledged that she felt comfortable and safe knowing he was available if help was required. He and Freddie exchanged words for some time and ended with each of them wishing the best to each other. Freddie could not have felt better knowing that his pal Enzo was there for his mother. It soon became time for them to retire. Freddie had a 4:00 a.m. appointment to keep. He bade his mother good night, gave her a hearty hug, and turned abruptly away. He did not want her to see the tears that were forming in his eyes.

The time to leave was upon him, and he was ready to follow Cole's instructions. Within a short period of time, he was off again to Husband Road for his transformation. Freddie Ryan walked into Cooper Smith's home and exited as Mike Sloan. He was then shuttled off to the Safe House in Marion, Illinois. The first thing he did was look in a mirror, searching for traces of his old self. They were not to be found. The make-up specialist knew what he was doing. He concurred with Cole that his own mother would not recognize him.

He didn't have much time to settle in before he headed off to his next destination. This time it was the new Swanson 's Supermarket in Marion. The hiring procedure was promptly taken care of, and he was soon finished with the orientation process and informed to report for work the next morning.

It was back to the Safe House where he was greeted by a female agent who spent several hours informing him of all that was required of him. He received pictures of individuals he was to be on the lookout for. She presented him with given codes to be used if conditions warranted the need. "Mr. Sloan, that is all that is requested of you. You are not to put yourself or any of the employees in danger by any actions you might take. Do you understand fully what I have related to you? It is imperative that my instructions are carefully followed. By not adhering to them, you could possibly jeopardize the operation. We do not have the luxury of permitting the drug dealers any more time to wreak havoc. Within the last two weeks it had been necessary to medically treat fourteen victims in order to save their lives. We can account for seven less fortunate users who were not so lucky. We have to stem the supply of these dangerous drugs before more fatalities are recorded. The area from Marion to Carbondale has become a hotbed of drug activity. We need your help."

The first day at work was spent in cashier training activities that would enable the trainees to successfully pass the required tests. Mike Sloan was a quick learner and had been assessed as ready to start cashiering the very first thing the next day. His total concentration the first couple of days was focused on what he had been taught to do. His mind was clearly concentrating on what the position demanded of him in order to remain in the cashier position.

The end of the week found him enjoying the job, liking his living quarters, and fully energized to stay on the physical training routine outlined for him. His keen sense of perception had allowed for him to concentrate on two individual employees. He was willing to bet his first weeks' pay that he had pegged each of them correctly. The first individuals bearing was perceived to be similar to that of Bruce Cannon, the Drug Enforcement Administration (DEA) plant working at the store in Paducah. He was to be the first person he wanted to get acquainted with. The other individual had a swagger about him that raised his suspicions. He wondered if this guy could be a part of the drug ring that was pushing drugs to vulnerable young people. He would become number two on his get acquainted list. A concern was developing.

The next week where Conor had been holed up, he witnessed an abundance of activity. He could account for seven visits being made in that span of time. On one of the occasions, several new individuals were dropped off, and the two who had been there since his arrival had departed. During that time period, he was trying to improve on his ability to eavesdrop on the many conversations taking place. It seemed to him that the new arrivals spoke louder and more distinctly. That was a welcome stroke of luck he definitely favored.

On one of the evenings when he was freed from his room to eat dinner he engaged in a brief conversation with one of the new additions. The guy seemed to invite dialogue from Conor who was starving for palaver with anybody. Conor took the opportunity to ask if he could possibly do some bird watching tomorrow afternoon. He advised that he was helping with the efforts but was being treated like a prisoner. "No harm can come from my enjoying what I like to do. I really need to have some sort of diversion. I am starting to go stir crazy being penned up in that room all day long. I would like to be able to talk to my wife to let her know that I am doing fine."

Mike was bored with the inactivity he was faced with at the store. He reflected on the fact that a drug agent's job could be very boring. Playing the waiting game was not something he found pleasure with. He wondered why the two people that he singled out seemed to have so much in common. In his estimation, they were not birds of a feather but did spend a lot of time together. What it was that they could have in common was highly puzzling to him. His visit with Rolf Bauer, the one who was patterned after Bruce Cannon, reinforced his feelings that there seemed to be a semblance of commonality between them. The sparse conversation he was able to get in with Jade Peters afforded very little to form any opinion of him. He just did not feel comfortable being around him. That was enough for him to remain wary and vigilant concerning Jade. He was of the opinion that it was going to take a lot longer to get a break in this case. That was not the outcome for which he had hoped. It was not at all to his liking.

The next couple of days had an up-tempo beat about them. He noticed repeat visits by several fellows. They seemed to spend an inordinate amount of time looking for what little they bought. It seemed to him that Rolf Bauer always made it a point to be nearby and focus his attention in their direction. Mike took the time to strike up light conversations with them as they progressed through the cashier station. There was very little repartee on their part and their actions signaled they were not in the mood for conversation of any kind. His purpose in doing so was to have them pause for a longer period of time. It would allow him to take note of their facial features and determine if they matched any of the people in the pictures that were given to him.

When the twosome had departed, Rolf meandered over to Mike's station and inquired of him, "Buddies of yours?" "Who are you talking about?" "The guys that just went through your line, you seemed to be familiar with them." "I have no idea who they might be. I like to make it a point to be friendly with all of the customers I check out. It is a good business practice, which might possibly result in return business and possibly regular customers. It's my insurance policy. There are no jobs where there are no customers." "I like the way you think." "Well thank you. It doesn't cost me a cent to do it. It's one of the first steps from Cashier to Store Manager." "Go tiger."

If things seemed to be up-beat for Freddie, they would have to be described as turbulent for Conor. Activity abounded. There were drop-offs, pick-ups, incessant telephone calls, and constant change of personnel. It did appear to him that more cases were coming in than were being taken out. He figured that situation would be to the dismay of the Big Dog.

It didn't take long for what he suspected to be confirmed. As he was sitting in his room, he was fortunate to have been able to overhear a louder than normal conversation that took place between the two ring members. "Max, it looks as if our efforts are not sufficient to please our Chicago comrades. I have become aware that they are making some loud noises over the issue." "There definitely is a breakdown somewhere, and there's nothing we can do to correct it. You can bet we will be read the riot act even though that is a fact. I don't know about you, but I get a little uneasy about what I see coming this way."

They were not the only ones that had an uneasy feeling about the state of affairs. Conor decided that he had better start doing something regarding the coding needs. Being prepared would make it so much easier to enter the necessary information as it became known to him. The immediate task at hand was to be able to have the book in his hand outside of his room. He had to get the watchdogs comfortable with the book, as well as his pretending to be making identifications of various species. The more they saw of this activity, the less likely his actions were to draw suspicion.

CHAPTER EIGHTEEN:

NO LULL BEFORE THE STORM

Cole and his group were finding things to be rather cyclonic themselves. They were engaged in a series of twists and turns that appeared to be capable of bearing fruit. Unfortunately, it seemed that their efforts were of no avail. They were constantly falling short of coming up with needed answers.

Just as it seemed that they had reached the end of the trail, a misfortune for the drug dealers turned out to be a stroke of luck for Cole and his men. A truck laden with drugs was supposedly being transported from the gulf coast of Mississippi to a location in St. Louis, Missouri and had broken down. When the local law enforcement came upon the scene, drugs were being shuttled from the broken-down vehicle to another. Quick action on their part enabled them to take the culprits into custody and seize whatever of the cargo had not been transferred. Several smaller trucks had already offloaded some of the drugs and were on their way delivering them to the intended destination. The police were advised by a local farmer, Mr. Brown, that two trucks had just left approximately five or so minutes ago. He had been watching from the porch of his home and was able to supply them with accurate descriptions of the vehicles.

Mr. Brown estimated that the broken-down truck had to wait four to five hours before the first of the smaller trucks came on the scene. The two men, the driver, and his passenger, had not left the big truck at any time while waiting for help to arrive.

An all-points bulletin was issued and law enforcement agencies throughout the area were alerted and issued orders on how to deal with the situation. Once the vehicles had been spotted, and verified to be the ones being sought, they were to be pursued to their destination. It was intended that the pursuing vehicles were to have no markings which would alert the fugitives they were being followed. All necessary precautions were to be taken in order not to raise suspicion of any sort.

Further orders stated that the pursuing vehicles should be manned with sufficient manpower and weaponry to deal with what may be a large number of felons at the delivery site. It was ordered for them to stay in touch by way of their two-way radio so that DEA agents could arrive in time to lend support. No action was to be taken before the agents arrived unless action had been initiated against them. It was also imperative that no harm come to a citizen who had been placed there by the agency. The arriving agents were aware of his identity. They were told to proceed with the utmost caution.

Back at the store, Rolf Bauer was sure that Jade Peters was spending an excessive amount of time at the receiving dock. He seemed to be engaged with several of the drivers from the various distributors that had come in to make deliveries. While observing the activities he concluded that the delivery drivers were engaged in loading quite a few cartons onto their trucks before departing. He was not able to determine if that was a normal happening in the process. The fact that two drivers from different suppliers were leaving with what appeared to be similar cartons was puzzling to him.

Freddie, AKA Mike Sloan, was concerned about two men who had entered the store, and without hesitation headed over to speak with Jade. They seemed to be having a guarded conversation that was very brief. The reason for coming to the store was taken care of and they exited promptly.

Two black sedans holding five passengers each were headed on a direct route to Southern Illinois. It was apparent that they were traveling together. They traveled at a rate of speed that would not attract attention, but that allowed them to push the limit a bit. Only one stop had been made, that being to use the comfort station. The passengers of both vehicles hurriedly loaded back into the cars. They were on a mission.

The activity at the house found Conor in the process of loading cases onto the back of a truck capable of hauling all the supply of drugs stored there. He was getting very little help in the process and his back was hurting considerably. The three goons who were there with him were concerned with keeping watch for uninvited guests. Every once in a while, one of them would inquire, "How are you doing, muscles?" Their orders were to have the truck loaded, and on the road to a destination in St. Louis, Missouri.

The truck was fully loaded, with the drop-down door closed and padlocked. The driver, who had been napping, was wakened, and told to hightail it to St. Louis immediately. One of the three that was there was chosen to ride shotgun to ensure safe delivery of the valued cargo. He was armed with what the Chicago boys referred to as a typewriter. The Thompson submachine gun he toted was capable of supplying ample firepower in the event of being pulled over by the police. The guard was carrying two spare one hundred round fully loaded drums of ammunition. Three hundred rounds of .45 caliber ammunition could cause a lot of damage in a short period of time.

Conor was hurting badly and had returned to his room to lie down in bed. He knew that things were not right and was concerned for his safety. The ex-DEA agent had not appeared on the scene, so he was left to fend for himself. There was not much in the way of defense that he could offer, being unarmed.

He was unaware that at this moment, gang members were converging on his location from the north and the south. While lying there he picked up on a conversation between the two remaining men. He heard one of them say, "You can stay here if you want, but I am hitting the road. I witnessed the big guy's temper tantrum once before. It does not end up being pretty. If we run now, we escape his wrath. Somebody is going to pay for the predicament that we are in right now. He is not picky. His motivation is to put a scare in everybody that if you screw up, you will answer for it."

Somebody in the organization had issued an order for the drug shipment coming from Mississippi to be delivered to the house in Marion. It was wrong information, as they were to be sent on to St. Louis, and to bypass Marion. Conor's only hope was that the misinformation causing the shipment to come to Marion would create enough confusion that he could slip out somehow. The chance of that happening was very unlikely.

Locating his bird book, Conor hurriedly entered a note in hopes that Maureen and Freddie knew how much he loved them. The note was scribbled in on the first page in the book. He would waste no time entering any code information. That information was of no value under the present circumstances. His thoughts had to be centered on one thing only, his survival. There were no regrets on his part regarding the decision he made to work with the DEA. Cole impressed upon him the potential danger that was inherent in the operation. *I am here, and I intend to do whatever is required of me.*

Cole and three of his agents were in Murphysboro, Illinois, a town about fifteen miles remote of

Carbondale. They were there on a tip received earlier in the day. The tip paid dividends for the agents, in that three suspected dealers were rounded up and taken into custody. They were also visited with a bit more of good luck. One of the three that were taken into custody wanted to talk with Cole in private, out of hearing range of his partners. Cole inquired, "What is it you wanted to talk about?" He proceeded to inquire, "If I were able to divulge some information which would be of interest to you, could you find a way to cut me some slack?" "I can't make any promises, but I assure you if your information turns out to be of help to us I will do all that I can to help you." "I overheard you saying to your men that you were bent on trying to intercept a load of drugs coming out of Mississippi. Your information has been that the drugs were on the way to St. Louis. If you were to make your move based on that, you would be heading away from where the drugs are actually bound for. We were just informed to head to Marion because the wrong destination was given regarding where they were to be delivered. Our job was to try to intercept the truck and divert it on to St. Louis. We most likely would be too late to deliver that information, as that truck has more than likely arrived there. I am glad that I was not the one to send the message wrongfully advising where to convey the cargo."

From all indications, it appeared Conor was correct in assuming there would be confusion. It would be much more accurate to state that the situation would soon become uncertain and dangerous. Three separate groups were converging on the house in Marion. The inbound truck was minutes away, the group out of Chicago were within forty minutes of arriving, and Cole and his agents were due within an hour. Conor was fraught with anxiety and had not come up with anything to help him get out of the house. Although there was only one accomplice left at the house, this did not make it any better for him. The one who had flown the coop was a reasonable individual and might have been of the nature to allow for Conor to be spared.

CHAPTER NINETEEN:

THE TEMPEST IS AT HAND

Before the storm was to hit, Conor was feverishly contemplating his moves. He knew he had no chance at convincing the lone gang member to let him escape. The man was a loyalist to the big guy and knew well if Conor was gone, he would be in deep trouble due to his absence. There was nothing in his room with which he could use as a weapon to defend himself. His deep abiding faith was all he had to bolster himself against the harm that might befall him. It was a grim situation he was faced with, and he was well aware the consequences could be direful.

It was not long before the southern group pulled in and soon found Conor in the act of unloading cases off of the first truck to arrive. He was about halfway through unloading when the two sedans coming out of Chicago made their entrance. Within seconds of their arrival the scene became a flurry of action. Orders were being yelled out to get the truck reloaded and to hit the road to St. Louis. The next words Conor heard were, "Where is that drug salesman at?" "He's the guy that has been unloading the truck." "Get him over here to me. I need to have a talk with him." Conor was brought face to face with the King Pin and realized the gravity of the situation. Sweat from unloading would soon be amplified due to his apprehension. "So, you are the cause of all of our problems. Do you realize what you have cost me in the way of lost sales? Do you have any idea as to how mad that makes me?" The big guy interrupted the conversation and yelled out again, "Get more guys on the loading operation. In fact, get this informant back to helping out. I'll deal with him once we get this stuff on the road to St. Louis."

Conor immediately returned to help reload the truck and minutes later the second truck arrived. The first truck had been reloaded and was sent on its way, along with the crew that came in on it and one of the sedans. Again, orders were barked out to get the second truck loaded and on the road.

While that was happening, the head man was grilling the one man that was left guarding the location. He was questioned as to why he did not have anybody with him. He replied, "I did have a partner who thought it was better to leave than incur your wrath. He was afraid that you might be upset about the state of affairs and possibly harm him." "Oh, harm will come to him alright. I will make sure of that. He won't have anywhere to hide from me. Why is it that you decided not to flee the coop with him?" "I am, and always have been, loyal to the operation and had no thoughts of bugging out." "I commend you for the decision you so wisely made. I do want you to know I am unhappy with how you handled... Hey, here comes a bunch of cars, it looks as if John Law has decided to join the party."

Cole and his vanguard came roaring in fully aware that there could possibly be some gunplay involved this eventful day. He, the DEA agents, along with several squads of State Patrolmen were on the run towards the house. Conor found this to be an opportunity to make his escape and took off on the run. His poor physical condition, due to all of the loading and unloading, did nothing to aid his efforts. He became an easy target for those from the sedan left behind. Before he could reach suitable cover, he heard a shot ring out and, in an instant, he felt a terrible burning sting in his right hip. He took a few more steps and fell to the ground. His assailant was neutralized in short order. One of the State Patrolmen was nearby and was able to get the shot off that helped level the odds. Conor, although hurt badly, was able to crawl to protective cover and was alert enough to apply compression to limit the bleeding.

Members of the drug ring were now holed up in the house and were spraying the surrounding area with gunfire. The one submachine gun that they had was getting full attention from the law officers. It appeared that the wielder of that piece of armament might have been hit. It was apparent that the staccato of his gun was absent from the fusillade being rained down on Cole and his men.

In a matter of seconds, the ring member being grilled by the King Pin made a break to pick up the weapon of the wounded man. Realizing that he had lost favor with the big guy, he scurried over to his position. His next move was to place the muzzle of the gun he was holding up against the back of his head. He disarmed him and advised him that he was to order all of his gang to cease fire and lay down their weapons.

The room, dense with gun smoke and the acrid fumes of gunpowder, suddenly quieted down. What sounded like the fireworks at a major Fourth of July celebration was met with dead silence. The three non-wounded members and their boss were instructed to raise their hands and to walk outside. They were greeted by the waiting lawmen gathered to take them into custody. The head man, who was none other than Diego Ruiz, was hurriedly cuffed, and placed in one of the agent's autos. Cole could not believe that they had snared a drug King Pin who had eluded capture for many years. His capture and the seizure of drugs over the last several days amounted to a major victory in the drug war.

The first order from Cole was to get to Conor and tend to his needs. An ambulance had been called for, and in the meantime, Conor was administered whatever aid the DEA agents and State Patrolmen were able to provide. He was immediately placed in the ambulance upon its arrival and the medics on board went right to work stabilizing him. Prior to the departure of the ambulance, one of the medics was able to report that all should be well with Conor. He felt that his life was in no apparent danger at the present time. Cole breathed a sigh of relief and ordered the captured felons to be properly bound and escorted to the County Jail in Marion. The felon who aided the police in the capture was separated from the others and sent on to a prison in Pontiac, Illinois. The squad cars were instructed to act as escorts and to not let anyone interfere with the convoy. He wanted all proper security measures to be taken until Ruiz was transported to the nearest Federal Prison. He ordered two guards, working eight-hour shifts, to be present 24 hours a day.

Maureen was called and was informed of Conor's condition. A police car was sent to the apartment to take her to the hospital where he had been taken. She arrived minutes prior to his being wheeled into the operating room for removal of the bullet lodged in his hip area. He would have to undergo some reconstructive surgery to repair bone damage. She was advised there was nothing life threatening involved in the procedure. The specialist performing the operation assured her that he would be back to his old self within a period of four to six months. The surgery that was to be rendered, along with the physical therapy prescribed, would provide for complete recovery.

Maureen sat in the waiting room to hopefully hear good news regarding the outcome. She was happy to have Conor back and felt that all would turn out well for him. Her thoughts migrated to her son, who she knew to be at National Guard training. She wondered how she would get this news to him. She was aware of the anxiety that Freddie suffered, worrying about his father's wellbeing. She reflected on how thankful she was for all that Enzo had done for her during this ordeal. With his help in purchasing needed grocery items, it enabled her to scrape up the necessary funds for rent and normal household expenses. Her mind was full of thoughts of gratitude for the good she had received thus far.

Meanwhile at the store in Marion, Jade Peters, who had been informed of the situation at the storage house was seeking out Rolf Bauers. He now knew Rolf to be a part of the DEA group who was in the process of breaking up the ring. He was going to make sure that he would not be a hindrance to his escape from the area. He was not going back to prison and Rolf Bauers was not going to be the one to put him there. Jade was in the back of the store making sure he had not left anything behind that could tie him to the drug operation. Being assured he had taken sufficient steps to avoid being implicated, he headed for the front of the store. As he was on the lookout for Bauers, he spotted him at the cashier station talking to Mike Sloan. Jade reasoned that Mike had a tie-in with Bauers and was also somebody that had to be dealt with.

Bauers turned and spotted Jade heading in his direction and prepared to accost him. Before he was able to make a move, Jade swiftly closed in on him and drew his pistol from inside the waistband of his trousers. Mike, alerted to the fact, came out from behind the cashier's station and made a move to disarm Jade. He violently swung at Jade's gun hand to knock the pistol free from his grip. At the same time Jade made a defensive move to avoid the oncoming blow. The result was that Mike hit both hand and pistol, causing Jade to fire a round at the floor. Bauers struggled with him to wrestle the gun free. As he was securing the gun, Jade pulled a knife and made wild attempts to carve him up. Mike, AKA Freddie, AKA Pug, sent a swift right hook to Jade's midsection, knocking him off of his feet and leaving him gasping for air. He was abruptly cuffed and brought to his feet, still feeling the effects of the punch that did him in. Freddie tried to ease the pain he was suffering from striking the pistol. The blow that put Jade down added to the discomfort he felt.

All necessary precautions were taken and the captured ring members and their leader, Diego Ruiz, were transported to the federal prison in Marion to await trial. After sentencing they were returned to serve their sentences out at Marion, the prison built to replace Alcatraz.

Cole finished wrapping up all necessary items, and a week later took the opportunity to visit Conor at the hospital. Conor was found to be in good spirits and was recovering nicely from his ordeal. From all indications there was no concern for possible complications to occur. Upon entering the hospital room he questioned, "Well, how is our hero doing? How do you feel, Conor?" "Hi Cole, thanks for the visit. I am feeling very well, thank you. I don't need the hero designation because it does not fit the situation." "Anybody who takes a .45 slug in this battle on drugs deserves that and much more. I am so glad to see you alive and doing well. Things could have turned out much worse for any one of us. I am sorry to say we lost one agent and had two wounded patrolmen in the firefight. We are so fortunate that one of the ring members marched the remaining gunmen out into our laps." "What happened to him?" "He will stand trial for his involvement in drug activity. I have provided much information that should favor him. More than likely, he will receive a lighter sentence. I sure hope so." "You certainly deserve appreciation and recognition for your doggedness in putting an end to that gang's activity." Cole interrupted Conor as he was about to deliver more laudits. "Let me give you some facts as to where we stand. That's a whole new subject."

"What we have accomplished is nothing more than a needle in a haystack. Sure, we put Ruiz behind bars along with eleven others. Seven of those were from the first truck to leave for St. Louis and the passengers in the sedan escorting them. Three had met the fate that they were used to dealing out and will no longer be able to do so. We recovered a good part of the illegal drugs they were trying to peddle. Unfortunately, we did not corral one of the trucks, as it had already left the house in Marion before we arrived. Thankfully, what we did intercept will never be used to poison the young and vulnerable for which they were meant. We rounded up several members from the two stores located in Paducah and in Marion. You, your wife, and son are all safe and well."

"That all probably sounds terrific to you, but it tells me we have so much more to do. Somebody will replace Ruiz, and new gang members will be added constantly. New shipments of drugs will arrive daily. It is a never-ending process. Ruiz will get paroled or finish out his whole sentence and be back at doing what he is used to doing. We won a minor victory, and still have a great war to be won. It will take a lot more victories before we can delight in and celebrate total defeat of a terrible plague. I end on a sad note informing you that the drug problem nationwide will only get worse. We have to modify our stance from reactive to proactive in order to stem the tide."

Cole bid him goodbye and wished him good luck in his new position with his company. "It could not happen to a better man and his wonderful family. You know where to find me should the need arise. So long hero."

CHAPTER TWENTY:

A NEW DAY IS DAWNING

The newspapers in Mississippi, Tennessee, Alabama, Illinois, and especially Kentucky were emblazoned with news regarding activities related to the drug bust. They featured stories that tied together all aspects of the successful outcome. What they did mostly was add a bit of color to what action took place in their respective states. There were articles about lucky breaks the law enforcement personnel were afforded. There was news about the truck breakdowns, desertions of members of the drug ring, the shootout, Conor's wounding, Mike's heroic actions, and especially the surrender at the storehouse. What was missing, and would never be told, was Freddie's contribution in the matter. It was reasoned that by spelling out his part in the matter, too many of the DEA's methods of operation would be exposed. They further reasoned that by doing so it could possibly expose identities of persons that contributed help or information to law enforcement.

Freddie returned from his supposed National Guard training and was focused on getting back to work. On a recent visit to the store in Marion to meet with Gloria Brooks, he was pummeled with well wishes from many of the store's personnel. He was astounded when Mr.

Fred Gaines came up to him to welcome him back from camp. Fred inquired, "Are you back to work now?" Freddie replied, "No, not yet. Ms. Brooks and I are still working out the details regarding that matter." While they were engaged in conversation, he wondered why Gaines had not been rounded up by the police. "Mr. Gaines, I find it a puzzle to me why I am getting so much attention from you when you did not see me fit to work in your department." "I can readily explain that to you. I wanted badly to have you in my department, but existing circumstances prohibited it. You see, I was trying to rehabilitate a group of youngsters that were leaning in the wrong direction. Among that group was an old nemesis of yours, Bruno Balicki, who you engaged in fisticuffs on several occasions. I was concerned that if I had both of you together, feathers might get ruffled again between you two. What I was trying to accomplish was to get these boys to walk away from fights, and I did not want to introduce the potential for a fight to develop." "I noticed Bruno looking over at me, but he had made no attempt to greet me." "I can tell you why. First of all, it is at his insistence that I am requesting you join in to help me in my program. Bruno is ashamed of the fact that his father, who is now in Federal Prison, has caused your family so much grief. I assure you he holds no enmity towards you. The fact is, he welcomes your participation. Are you ready to join and help me?" "I am interested, but I want to see if I can fit that in with what I am trying to accomplish. Once I put the puzzle together, I will come to see you. One last question. Why are you meeting in the back of a grocery store?" "We had nowhere else to go and we could not afford to rent anyplace. Mr. Swanson heard of what I was trying to accomplish and granted permission to use the space." "Wow, I find that rather strange that he would do so." "When you have been there yourself and realize the grief that can be caused from lack of structure and guidance, it probably made it easy for him to make the offer. At the present time, he is reeling from almost being terminated by a member of the drug ring. That guy, Rocco, is now the recipient of free government housing in Marion. I hope I have not scared you away from joining me." "Not a bit."

Conor's recovery was progressing ahead of anticipated schedule. He was formally granted a promotion along with a sizeable increase in salary, requiring relocation to South Carolina. Maureen was kept busy making preparations for their impending move within the next three to four months. Freddie planned on staying in Paducah until he determined his direction in life. He was in search of and yearned for stability at his young age. There was no need or real reason for him to pursue his intentions of becoming a prize fighter.

Freddie and his friend, Enzo, had been practically inseparable since his return. On what turned out to be a beautiful Saturday morning, they were found to be on the way to their favorite gym. It was Freddie's first opportunity since his return to wind his way over to see his old friend B.J.. B.J. was anxiously waiting to see him, knowing for sure that the two of them would be coming by.

CHAPTER TWENTY-ONE:
IN SEARCH OF AN IDENTITY

Enzo and Freddie arrived at the gym and were greeted warmly by the owner. The questions were flying off of B.J.'s tongue faster than Freddie could reply. The one big and expected question eventually surfaced as he was asked, "Are you ready to return to the routine of preparing yourself for your involvement in the boxing game?" "I knew that question would be coming. Our financial problem has been solved and we are no longer in need of money that would have come from some early boxing matches. You may remember that I was anxious to get involved because we were in a financial bind. Now that the need no longer exists, I am taking the time to determine what I want to do with my life." "That is a good idea. Do keep in mind that you have the ability to become a World Champion. Of that I am sure. You could weave your aspirations together and achieve more than one goal. You must already know that I am here for you whenever you decide to resume training." "I just need a little time to think about the matter." Before leaving the gym that day, Freddie, and Enzo engaged in their normal routines. While banging away at the speed bag Freddie avoided using his right hand as much as he could. That fact did not go unnoticed by the keen eyes of B.J.. When leaving he was questioned as to why he was favoring his right hand. In reply he stated, "I slightly injured it in one of the training exercises while at National Guard training." "Did you report it?" "No, but I did see a doctor here. He prescribed some therapy routines that I am faithfully performing." "The next time you come in I would like to have a look at it." "Sure enough, medicine man. So long for now, see you next Saturday." "You take care of yourself."

The two compadres enjoyed their day together as usual. They didn't do anything special, just hung out and enjoyed each other's company. Freddie felt he owed a debt of gratitude to Enzo for all that he did for his mother while at camp. This made parting difficult for him, but he had to say goodbye for now. He was eager to get home to spend as much time with his parents as possible. It would not be much longer that he would be able to be with them.

It was a wonderful evening of conversation and togetherness that was enjoyed by all three of them. Freddie and Conor found some time to play several hands of cribbage. Maureen was kept busy fixing some snacks for the two competitors. The outcome found the son beating his father two out of three games. They spent a good deal of time discussing the impending move and figuring out plans for meetings on a regular basis. It soon came time to bid each other goodnight, and off to bed they went.

They were greeted with a beautiful, sunny Monday morning and were engaged in conversation when the phone interrupted them. The call was for Freddie and his mom handed him the phone. "Hello, this is Freddie." "Good morning, Ms. Brooks here. How are you this fine morning?" "I am doing great, it's nice to be hearing from you." "I am calling with good news for you." "And that is?" "The check for your back-pay has arrived. I would like it very much if you could come in to meet with me tomorrow. I would like to hand you the check personally. I would also like to get you back to work now that you have settled in after your training stint. Could you come in at 10:00 a.m. tomorrow?" "I can be there. I do want to talk to you about going back to work." "Okay, I hope you are not having a problem about coming back." "No, none at all. See you tomorrow."

"Mom and Dad, that was Ms. Brooks. The check for my back-pay is at the store. I am going there tomorrow to pick it up. She also wants to set me up to get back to work. The check along with my weekly pay should enable us to pay our expenses without any problem." Maureen could not hold back her admiration for her son and made him aware of how proud she was of him. "Son, I can't express how grateful your father and I are for all that you are so willing to do for us. It will not be forgotten, and we will repay you once we get our lives back on track." "That won't be necessary. I am happy that I am able to help out."

Freddie spent the rest of the day contemplating what position he would like to work at upon his return. While under the guise of Mike Sloan, he learned to enjoy his work as a cashier. He especially liked the interactions he had with the many customers he served.

He also enjoyed the time he spent in the customer service area, and really thought highly of his boss. It appeared that his choice would most likely direct him to working in the Grocery Department. After all, that was where he wanted to work when he was originally hired. The motivating factor in making that choice laid with the fact that he would be more readily available to work on Fred Gaines' project.

On the way to the store the next morning, the same exuberant feeling he had had on his first day of work there suddenly came over him. Life could not be better. He would be back to work. The fact that it enabled him to help his parents was the frosting on the cake. He was walking on air; he was on top of the world. Life was good.

Arriving at the store, he proceeded to go directly to Ms. Brooks' office and did not encounter any employees. Ms. Brooks greeted him warmly and asked him to have a seat. She appeared to be very relaxed and completely satisfied in her work. It was a noticeably different Ms. Brooks, very much unlike the one that he had seen on earlier visits. She presented him with his check and seemed to be more excited over the transaction than he was. He was deeply appreciative of the efforts she had taken to make it happen. His thoughts were focused on how much good the funds were going to do towards helping his parents. After the normal formalities were completed, Gloria asked him, "What is it that you want to find yourself doing here now? Do you want to go back to your old position, or do you want to learn new functions? You like contact with customers, maybe you might like to start with cashiering?" "I like your suggestion, but I would really like to start in the Grocery Department." "That's a strange request knowing that Mr. Gaines turned you down once before." Her unawareness of Fred Gaines' recent meeting with Freddie left her befuddled regarding his request. *Why would he want to be let down again? Was he intentionally setting himself up to be disappointed once more?* She cautioned him, "You know there is the possibility that Fred may once more reject you." "I feel that he would welcome me this time. A conversation I had with him a week ago alerted me that he would be open to accepting me in his department." "Oh, I wasn't aware of your visit with him. Hang loose while I get him to come to the office. Would you like a cup of coffee while we wait?" "No thanks, Mr. Gaines does not think too highly of spending time drinking coffee. I don't want to present a bad second impression."

Fred Gaines came in and wasted no time greeting both Gloria and Freddie. He inquired, "Mr. Ryan, nice to see you again. How are you doing? How is your hand?" "Not one hundred percent but I am pleased with the progress thus far. I would expect that with another month of Physical Therapy, I should be close to being totally mended." "That is good to hear. How soon can you start to work?" "Tomorrow would be fine with me." Gloria stood with her mouth wide open and bewildered about what had just transpired. She was under the impression that she would have to engage in a selling effort in order to effect this outcome. She didn't even have time to tell Mr. Gaines his reason for being called to her office. Fred, aware of her confusion, quickly explained the whole situation to her. "I thought that I had sufficiently explained my reasons for rejecting him the first time. I either was a bad presenter of the facts, or you were not an engaged listener on that occasion." "I would confess the predicament I was faced with at the time found me not operating on all cylinders. I accept that I was not a good listener. I would say at this time I am so happy about how everything played out. It was good fortune on everybody's part that a Swanson's employee, Mike Sloan, played such a heroic role in helping set things straight. The sad part of it is that Mr. Sloan has not been back to work since that incident. He has not responded to any of the attempts made to contact him. I find that to be very strange behavior on his part. The best part of all is that we have Freddie back with us. I see a great future for him here at Swanson's. Thank you, Fred. Welcome back Freddie. See you all at work tomorrow."

Freddie enjoyed the next month, getting to know his job and helping Mr. Gaines in his work with wayward youth. The rehabilitation project proved to be very rewarding to him, and he enjoyed all of the time and effort he put into it. The only concern was the lack of a nice welcoming space to work with the young men. His feeling was that more could be accomplished with a location offering comfortable seats and homey furnishings. It would offer a safe place the group could call their own, and to spend leisure time.

Freddie spent little time giving thought to resuming training with B.J. He was constantly focusing his energies trying to find a suitable location. One day as he was sitting and stewing over his lack of progress in the matter, a light bulb went off. *Why couldn't we do this at the gym?*

The next day he ambled over to the gym in order to present the question to a person longing to be his fight manager. He explained his dilemma to B.J. and plunged right in to asking, "Do you think you might be interested in housing our group until we find a suitable location?" He would receive an answer that did not solve his problem at all. "No, champ, I do not see how that would be possible without hurting my business. There just is not enough room in here. I am afraid it would bother my clients and possibly cause some of them to leave. I am sorry that I am unable to say yes to your reasonable request. There are circumstances in play that are not to my liking. I will share them with you, but they are to remain confidential. Do you agree to keeping them so?" Freddie quickly assented with a nod of his head.

B.J. goes on to say, "I am having some health issues. At the present time they are not bothersome, but they will become so. I am advised to avoid over-exertion and stress, as these trigger reactions that aggravate the problem. I also am having some financial difficulties due to some unpaid taxes from years back. I am being assessed penalties and interest is building, making things very uncomfortable for me. That of course is causing stress that I cannot control. I am going to have to raise membership fees or increase membership in order to be able to stay afloat. It is not a good place that I find myself in presently. I don't have answers, but I do have need for them." "I sure don't have the wherewithal or the answers you are seeking. One thing you can be assured of is that I will be looking for the answers you need. I will do everything I possibly can in order to help you. I am so sorry to hear of your problems, especially those concerning your health. Please don't hesitate to ask me for help where you think I might be able to offer some. I will see you Saturday. You know how to get ahold of me if you should need something sooner. You have my phone number. It is in the book under my dad's name if you can't find your note. So long for now, remember I am here to help. Don't be afraid to ask."

On his arrival at home, he was the recipient of some good news regarding his father's recovery progress. The doctor was quite pleased with how well his healing was coming along. The doctor felt that at the rate he was healing he might possibly be able to release him a month earlier than originally anticipated. Freddie was delighted to hear the good news but did not like the inevitable result from it. It very well could mean that his parents would be moving earlier than scheduled. He readily accepted the good news, but their moving earlier would be a bitter pill to swallow. It seemed to him that sad events come in bunches sometimes.

He had a night of disturbed sleep due to what was added to his plate. It was bad enough they would be leaving, now it turned out it would possibly be sooner.

He was somewhat reconciled to the first departure date and now was revisited with knowing it more than likely would be earlier than planned. He tossed and turned over B.J.'s plight invading his thoughts alternately. He said he was available to him for help. He now realized he did not even have an idea of what kind of assistance he could offer. He knew the earlier departure of his parents, although unwelcome, would be dealt with. The real quandary he was faced with was what he could do to for his friend, who was in need of his help.

On the way to work he was revisited with thoughts of the predicament that B.J. was faced with. He knew that he had no one to turn to in order to seek help. Freddie was thoroughly convinced that he had to come up with the answers to solve his friend's problems. In his search for solutions his very first thought was to rethink his position regarding the fight game. He reasoned it was the only way he knew of that he would be able to get the cash that was needed. The time it would take to complete his training could possibly be four to five months. It would require good fortune to be able to secure a match before the lapse of six months. If he were to be matched with an up-and-comer, his part of the purse would be more than he could earn in the span of a year. He questioned whether his right hand would allow for this to happen.

While at the store his thoughts shifted to his concern of losing the opportunities he felt were available to him at Swanson's Supermarket. He knew there was a lot of thinking that needed to be applied before he would

make a final decision. It was a heavy load that he had
suddenly become burdened with.

CHAPTER TWENTY-TWO:

DECISION MAKING TIME

There was little time for procrastination on his part. Too much was at stake. While in the process of determining the right move, he reflected on his prior pugilistic experiences. He recalled that he was an unwilling combatant in his early years due to his mother's dislike for that activity. There were recollections of fights he was involved in simply because his opponents felt he was easy prey. Then there were the times when he became involved in order to come to someone's aid. It was painful for him to remember the difficulties it cost him in finding employment. There was nothing that he could think of that would endear him to becoming a prize fighter.

He mused on the fact that just a short time ago he was training for the purpose of becoming a boxer. There was definitely satisfaction derived from some of his training activity, and he was savvy regarding techniques and strategy. B.J., who was willing to train him, saw considerable promise for his success. It was safe to say that he saw in him the potential to become a champion at it. There were considerable positives that could motivate him to jump at the challenge.

What concerned him was the lack of motivation he
exhibited in continuing on with his training. He could
only figure that his reason for not participating in the
sport was his concern for injuring an opponent. He
concluded that he flat-out disliked being involved, but
all of those thoughts needed to be dispelled. It was time
to assume a purpose of resolve and commit to what was
required of him.

That evening he sat down with his father and discussed
what was rattling through his mind. His father was an
ardent listener who absorbed all that Freddie had to
offer. He did not hesitate to inform him that what he
was considering carried the potential for causing
serious injury to himself. He added that what Freddie
intended to do in the way of helping B.J. was an
unselfish act of kindness. "You know son, you have one
life to live. While doing so you want to make sure of
several things. You should derive pleasure from what
you do. Always strive to become the best you can be at
whatever you choose to do. Helping someone in need
can bring much satisfaction to you. Sometimes there are
unseen rewards that come to you as a result of your
actions. It behooves one to make sure that the course
he takes, is an honorable one. I am completely satisfied
in knowing that you will make the right decision. You
have done so all of your life and it is ingrained in you
to do the right thing. The decision is yours, and yours
alone. The rewards or repercussions, whatever they may
be, are yours to own. I pray that there will only be
rewards forthcoming from the course you take."

Saturday was upon him in a hurry. It was time for Enzo and him to enjoy another good day together. He informed Enzo that he would be spending considerable time with B.J. today. "I want to discuss the possibility of getting back into training." "Are you seriously thinking of getting into the sport?" "I have been giving it some thought this past week. My mind is not made up yet. There are some conclusions I have arrived at, and now I need to have B.J. affirm them. I want to give my decision as much consideration as I can muster. I am interested in what feedback B.J. has to offer." "Are you open to hearing my opinion?" "Absolutely, I have the utmost interest in what it is you have to offer." "I will start by saying that I have a grave concern about what you are proposing to do. You are not doing it because of the love of the profession. You know that, and I know that. We also both know the reason why. The concern I have is that your heart won't be in it, and it might lead to you getting badly injured. Your right hand is an issue and may not be sufficiently healed in order to absorb the force of consistent punches you throw. I am worried about you. You have to change your outlook, and know that you are going in to win, and not become a punching bag for your opponents. I hopefully wish for my comments to be helpful and not confuse you in your decision-making process." "I have heard everything you had to offer, and I am genuinely thankful for your concern. You can be sure that I will give utmost consideration to your advice. See you in a bit."

The conversation he had with B.J. echoed what he had just heard from his good friend. He was told that if his purpose was to raise money to help him out of a problem, he would not be a party to the plan. "Freddie, I have told you more than once that I believe you have what it takes to become a champion. I am telling you now, loud, and clear, something you need to know. You will not survive in this game unless you devote your whole self to desiring to be a winner. I will not train and arrange matches for somebody I do not believe in. You have to put your heart, mind, and body into everything you do from the moment I say we will do it together. I have no desire in leading a lamb to slaughter. So, as the saying goes, the ball is in your court. You tell me when you have your act together."

Freddie had one question he felt was deserving of an answer, "What effect will the effort you put into the training process have on your health?" "None at all if you prove to me that you are in for the purpose of becoming the best that you could be. If you give the impression that you are not, for me to continue, would cause undue stress that I do not need. I believe under the right set of circumstances this journey could become a source of good medicine for me." "One last question, do you think the timetables I have set are reasonable?" "I do believe they are achievable. What will be the determining factor is whether I think you are ready for the ring. I am not pushing you out there until I am satisfied you are reflecting the look of a winner. Incidentally, I would like a look at that hand of yours. Keep performing the exercises that were recommended, and let's both sleep on what we have talked about.

When you are ready to make the decision to go ahead, we will establish a new training routine and get the show on the road." "Will it require full-time attention on my part? I am asking if I have to give up my day job?" "I would have to say absolutely you do. You are going to have to eat, sleep, and think about what you are trying to achieve." "Get the routine ready. I will be requesting a leave of absence from work which will most likely require two weeks' notice. My folks will be leaving here shortly, so you can figure we start two weeks from this coming Monday. I want to spend the Saturdays before then being entirely devoted to them. I am all in."

After spending a nice weekend with his parents, he realized that these precious moments with them would soon come to an end. It was off to work again. Freddie was suffering from anxiety as to how his request for a leave of absence was going to turn out. It found him to be in complete turmoil. Leaving the job at this point could jeopardize his career chances with Swanson's after his boxing days were finished. His decision to go ahead with his training had to be his only focus right now. He knew well the direction he had to take.

Arriving at the store, he immediately strode over to Ms. Brooks' office to inform her of his decision. After listening to all he had to provide, she hesitantly advised him of her regret to see him leave. She also regretted that under the circumstances, a leave of absence could not be granted. "Freddie, I can only grant a leave for a maximum of thirty days. If you are intent on leaving, it will be based on your request for termination. I will accept your termination to be effective two weeks from now if that is your decision. This I can tell you, the opportunity for you to return will always be there. In your case, the physical state you are in upon returning will be the deciding factor." "I kind of figured that would be the case. I understand fully the reasoning behind it. I regret leaving but I have made my mind up. May I have a Request for Termination form please."

The rest of the day, and the rest of the remaining time was bittersweet for him. He was going to miss working there and would miss a lot of the friends he had come to know during his brief tenure. Although a lot was not expected from him, he worked diligently all through his last fourteen days. Mom and Dad were to be the recipients of his undivided attention until the day they would depart. He was not going to let anything interfere with his devotion to both of them. They packed a lot of living into those days, and regretted there could not be more of them.

Until the time for their leaving, he would train Monday through Friday. Saturday would be dedicated to spending time with his mom, dad, and Enzo. Sunday was strictly set aside for his folks. There would be no other way. The die had been cast. There was not to be any vacillation on his part.

The sad day arrived when he had to say goodbye to his folks. This would be the final separation for the Ryan family. It was hard for everyone to say goodbye, but inevitably the time had arrived. Hugs and kisses, words of sorrow, and words of encouragement were exchanged. Along with those were promises of seeing each other from time to time at the designated meeting place. The final waves were swapped as the car slowly pulled away. Tears were flowing freely from all of their eyes. The final curtain had come down on what had been loving family life for nineteen wonderful years.

CHAPTER TWENTY-THREE:

IT IS TIME TO DON THE GLOVES

There would be no more dilly-dallying. The time had arrived to get down to serious training. Freddie had promised himself that he would be fully dedicated to becoming a champion in the sport. Now that he was unemployed, and his parents had left for South Carolina, he could focus all of his attention on getting the job done.

As he had promised, on Monday morning he arrived at the gym energized and happy to get the ball rolling. He needed no coaxing to jump into the rigorous routine that would fill the next five long months. Under the watchful eye of his trainer, he performed all that was necessary to make B.J. a man of his words. He accomplished exactly what the sign above the gym door promised. He was a boy turned into a man.

His efforts each and every day were producing a well-defined and chiseled body. His every move was lightning fast, and his punches were getting to be unwelcomed by the sparring partners. The fact of the matter was that sparring partners were getting hard to find.

During those months, he learned to move like a ballerina. B.J. impressed upon him that strong legs and nimble footwork were the key to being the one standing after a bout. He was taught how to properly execute footwork featuring a slide step followed by several quicker steps. It was what would allow for smooth defensive and offensive movements. Months were dedicated to practicing the transition from defensive to offensive positioning. In that time, his every move was choreographed to prepare him for his first dance in the ring. There was not a single bit of information he would need to enhance his potential for victory that was not covered.

His run schedule was now calling for ten miles, much of which was done while throwing punches at the air. It seemed he could run as fast backwards as forwards. He would frequently change his direction, losing little speed while doing so. His running mates were constantly looking for the pace car to hop a ride. They could not keep up the pace. The guy was seemingly becoming superhuman.

B.J. became increasingly impressed with almost every aspect of Freddie's newly acquired talents. Although he was very adept at almost every part of the game, there were aspects which required some fine tuning. He developed a tendency to turn his toes in when transitioning, which left him unbalanced. The move took away precious moments and left him vulnerable to his opponent. It also deprived him of the opportunity to be able to launch decisive counterpunches after parrying the punches aimed at him. You could hear his trainer bellowing out, "Footwork, footwork," at his slightest miscue. He was constantly being told that the slightest slipup could open him up to an unwanted barrage. Until he could master that part of the game his only time in the ring would be with sparring partners. B.J. was adamant that he would not schedule a match until every little imperfection was eliminated. He had standards that had to be met. His desire to train a champion was being overridden by his need to have his fighter able to do all he required of him. He was not going to accept any flaw that needed to be corrected. B.J. did not want him to be permanently handicapped because he did not demand the best from him.

CHAPTER TWENTY-FOUR:

PATIENCE IS IN SHORT SUPPLY

Freddie was overly anxious and becoming bored with his training routine. It was not due to repetitive routines because that was not the case. B.J. had him spar with different mates daily. He wanted Freddie to get used to the differing styles that the sparring mates would present. He even allowed for the sparring mate to clinch longer than the allowable time in order to rile him up a bit. He tried everything allowable, especially one thing Freddie disliked. He did not like a swarmer or what is referred to as an infighter. A technical boxer such as him considered them to be a nightmare. He was sure to run into an opponent fitting that description and now was the time to figure out how to deal with the situation. He learned that by constantly throwing punches you deter his ability to enter your space. They did not have to be haymakers, only hard enough to sting and ward him off. He was slowly developing the arm strength necessary to deliver a prolonged salvo.

B.J. was also concerned about improving on Freddie's ability to disengage when tied up in a clinch. He spent considerable time training him how to get out of a clinch and delivering an uppercut as soon as his arm was freed. It would benefit Freddie in his near future to have had such an ardent taskmaster.

In Freddie's next sparring match, he was paired with a talented partner who was adept at forcing his opponents into the ropes. This matching made it possible for B.J. to instruct him in all of the strategies that would be valuable to him when backed up against the ropes. He was taught how to defend against repetitive blows allowing the aggressor to tire himself out. He was instructed how to bob and weave, thereby depriving his opponent of an easy target. One important lesson enlightened him how to be the aggressor on the ropes. He learned the art of keeping cool and how to use the ropes to his advantage. He would not be at a disadvantage if he employed the various strategies the situation warranted.

Training continued with B.J. exacting the maximum effort out of Freddie in each successive session. He was feeling quite confident of his pupil's abilities, but there would be no let-up in his training. There was a lot more he had to learn. He was learning each day that boxing required somewhat of a scientific approach to the game. He was introduced to differing offensive techniques as well as defensive moves that he would be confronted with. B.J. was intent on focusing on everything that might be detrimental and that could diminish his abilities. "Freddie, boxing is a sport that requires rigid discipline, your mind constantly engaged, and alert, a controlled temper, and your heart committed to what needs to be accomplished. You are going to be toe to toe with someone who has the same intentions as yours. He wants you down on the canvas for the count. To be the one standing you have to be the better one of the two. You need to be able to give and take, and you have to have a finisher's attitude. That means you cannot let up at any time and allow your opponent back into the fight. It's either you or him. You have to make sure that it is you who claims the victory. Remember that the fellow you will be pitted against has to play by the same rules as you do. Go into the ring being respectful of his abilities and aware of his weaknesses. Be smart and confident and a clean fighter and you will prevail."

Another month of rigorous training ensued and B.J. was confident that Freddie was in peak condition, had the motivation to win, and was hankering for that first bout. He was not going to engage him in the pro ranks right out of the gate. The first bout on the agenda would be non-professional. He was going to enter him in the Golden Gloves Organization.

All of the preliminary needs were satisfied within a two-week period. He was registered with Boxing USA, and had a bout set up with Golden Gloves. His first bout was set to take place in Ashland, Kentucky in two weeks' time.

The monotony of the training led Freddie to lose some of the sharpness he had worked so hard to perfect. B.J. was not going to allow for that to happen and set the tone for some very strenuous training. "Keep in mind, champ, you have a scheduled bout in two weeks, and I want you at the peak of your physical condition. I am not going to let you get soft before your inaugural fight. Get in that ring and wear those legs of yours out sharpening up your footwork. I want a winner going in and coming out of that ring. Polished footwork is going to be necessary to make that happen."

CHAPTER TWENTY-FIVE

IT'S PREP TIME

The day had arrived for Freddie's first bout, a three-round bout, with what appeared to be an evenly matched opponent. It was the first of three bouts that would ultimately lead him to a five round championship bout. A confident Freddie climbed up into the ring and did not appear to have any sign of jitters or concern. All of the preliminary instructions regarding Golden Glove Organization rules and regulations had been dispensed with prior to the bout. Without any further formality, the two boxers were advised to touch gloves and return to their corners.

The bout was taking place in familiar surroundings for Freddie as B.J.'s gym had been awarded official status as a Golden Glove Organization site. With this being the case, some minor modifications were made in order to accommodate approximately fifty spectators. Due to the size, his site did not meet the standards necessary to accommodate Regional Championship events. Fortunately, the location made it possible for some of Freddie's fans to be in attendance for the bout. Leading an entourage from Swanson's Supermarket were good friend, Enzo, Mr. Swanson, and Ms. Black, along with six other associates. Another group led by Fred Gaines and Bruno Balicki added twelve more to the fans present. This was especially pleasing to him. The fans attending for his opponent were about a half of that number. It would be the last time he would fight where all of the seats were not taken.

Prior to the start of the bout, B.J. told his warrior, "You have trained well for this occasion. Use what you have learned, and you will be victorious." It was fight time and the referee shouted out, "Come out fighting," and they did exactly that. Both fighters wasted no time in throwing leather, a lot of punches wild of the mark and ineffective. There did not seem to be much finesse exhibited by either fighter, which definitely did not escape the attention of B.J.'s keen boxing sense. The end of the round sounded, and two tired boxers headed to their seats in their corners for much needed rest.

The trainers wasted no time excitingly issuing instructions. In Freddie's corner he was getting an earful from his trainer. "You are not utilizing what you have been taught. Move around, anticipate his moves, be patient, feel him out, and then determine your strategy. Be yourself."

The second round started out much differently than the first. Freddie was moving around much more. He would move in and then out, causing some confusion for his opponent. This action saw his opponent eager to carry the fight to Freddie. He was a bit too eager, allowing Freddie the opportunity to land a combination of cross punches to the head which floored his opponent. He quickly recovered at the count of four, was back on his feet, and was again struck with a left hook to the body. The blow again saw him on the canvas. This time he was unable to answer. He took the count, resulting in a victory for the local hero.

All of his fans were ecstatic over his win, and greeted him with, "Attaboy, champ. You are the best." They all gathered around to congratulate him on his victory. He wanted mostly to get to the dressing room away from his admirers. He wanted to be away from all of the commotion that embarrassed him. Enzo informed the group it was necessary for him to return to be checked out by the doctor. A grateful young man headed for the dressing room for the calm he was seeking.

Two more matches remained before the upcoming championship fight, which he earned by defeating all three of his opponents. In the first of the two remaining bouts, he unknowingly struck his opponent in the liver, ending the bout. The blow to his opponent rendered him incapable of continuing on with the second round. With this type of injury, the pain is so severe that the person is often incapacitated. Most of the time, it results in a technical knockout. Such was the case that ended this bout. Freddie's first reaction was that he had committed a foul. It was not his intention to target the liver, and he felt very bad about the incident. As soon as he realized that his adversary had recovered, he made his way over to him and apologized. In the third or last bout prior to the championship match, his opponent was no match for the tiger that was unleashed that evening. The bout went all three rounds, all of which found Freddie winning by points. It was a wonder the losing fighter was capable of staying on his feet. In round two as well as three it appeared that the referee was about to stop the match and award a TKO to Pug. It was a testament to the durability and fortitude of his opponent.

CHAPTER TWENTY-SIX:

ASHLAND, HERE WE COME

The big night had finally arrived, and he found himself in Ashland, Kentucky to fight for the Golden Gloves Welterweight Championship of his region. His emotions were running wild. He was exhilarated by all the hustle and bustle of the relatively large crowd that filled the gymnasium in Ashland. At the same time, he was concerned and bewildered by the fact that he was again going into the ring to engage in fighting. His parents were not in attendance, and he wondered if his mother would really want to be there. He reflected on some of his past encounters, especially the one he had early on with Bruno Balicki. He knew this fight had a purpose to it. He wanted so much to get on with making some money in the game so that he could help out a cherished friend. He wondered if he would make him proud tonight.

B.J. was a bundle of nerves. He relished the fact that he was privileged to have the opportunity to train and manage a youngster with so much talent. His every thought was for the concern of the safety of his boxer. He did not want anything untoward to happen to a young lad he felt was his own son. He thought, why in the world he had hung the title "champ" on him and kept mentioning to him that he had the makings of a champion. Was he the one responsible for his being here tonight?

It was not long before a knock on the door came along with the announcement that it was fifteen minutes till fight time. There was no longer any time for wondering and worrying about happenings in the past. Now was the time for both of them to focus on what was needed to compete and win. The next several minutes were spent shoring up Freddie's confidence and rehashing what little they knew about the competitor's boxing abilities and style. They did know this much; Stanley the Brawler Kowalski was a formidable opponent who had a string of six victories going for him. Three of those were by way of a knockout. He wielded a mighty right-hand punch and had used it in all of his knockouts. Pug had to be aware of that and to fight an evasive fight while waiting for the right time to carry the fight to Kowalski.

The next knock on the door was for the purpose of advising them that it was time to proceed to the ring. It was fight time. A nervous B.J. led his boxer down the aisle to engage in his first championship match of his career. Freddie Pug Ryan showed signs of a confident fighter who had been through this ritual many times before. He was ready to perform knowing full well that he was competently trained for this eventuality. He had the best trainer in the country along with a loyal corner man waiting to attend to him. He felt even better now once he saw his favored friend, Enzo, waiting to spread the ropes for him to make entry into the ring. Unknown to Freddie, Enzo had been engaged in training sessions learning how to deal effectively with cuts sustained during a match. He would be handling the duties of a corner man as well as a cut man this evening. The next time Freddie was booked for a fight, Enzo would also be the one who would be taping his hands, readying him for the event. His presence as a corner man would play well for the benefit of the young boxer.

CHAPTER TWENTY-SEVEN:

THE FIGHT IS ON

Upon entering the boxing ring, Freddie was occupied eyeing his opponent and wondering if his right hand was as effective as they had said it was. He danced around in his corner while feigning punches he randomly threw into the air. Continually moving, he watched carefully as his opponent moved about, paying particular attention to his footwork. He became aware of the fact that Kowalski had a tendency to turn in his right toe when feigning a right cross. He registered that in his mind as something that might benefit him during the match.

He was not too engaged that he didn't take the time to occasionally glance over to his corner to eye his trainer and corner man. He could not be more thrilled knowing he had two trusty friends in his corner. He reflected on the reason for his being here that evening, and how important it was for him to succeed in the boxing game. He had a dear old friend who was in need of help, and he was the one to fill that need.

Now it was time to focus on all that his esteemed trainer had taught him in all those long months of training. He recalled B.J.'s instructions to continually anticipate his opponent's next move, and how to react to them. His mind was a flurry of all of the many bits of advice he had been given.

There was no more time left for thinking of things in the past. It was time for one thing only, to keep his mind on what was at hand. The two gladiators were summoned to the middle of the ring by the referee. They were questioned as to whether they remembered the information he had previously given to each of them. Upon their affirmation of the fact, they were directed to touch gloves, fight a clean fight, and return to their respective corners. Before the first round was to begin, Freddie was greeted with well wishes from B.J. and Enzo. The referee called out, "Fighters come out to do what you came here for and fight clean."

The fight was on. Freddie was greeted with a stinging left hand, which prompted him to realize Kowalski also had a mean jab. It didn't take anything more than a second to know he was in for a fight. They both danced around a bit until Freddie saw an opening to return the favor. It did not have the same effect as the one he was greeted with. His opponent's bobbing and weaving was making him a difficult target. Another left from Freddie and Kowalski's right hand was there to deflect it. Fortunately, his right cross found it's mark in his midsection, causing Kowalski to wince and back away. A little more evasive movement on the part of his opponent and soon the bell signaling the end of round one sounded. Both fighters retreated to their respective corners where they were given advice by their trainers.

Round two was a little more robust, finding both fighters exchanging some rather punishing volleys. In one of the exchanges, Freddie was on the receiving end of a blocked left jab followed by a solid right to the side of his jaw. His ability to turn away from the punch took away the effect that the punch was meant to impart. He did notice that Kowalski was turning in his right toe. It confirmed what he had noticed prior to the fight. The effect of doing so impeded his ability to recover quickly in order to defend himself from punches thrown at him. The bell ending round two had sounded.

Back in his corner, Freddie received a stern warning that he had to defend himself from that punishing right hand of his opponent. If he were to win this fight, he was going to have to be more aggressive while at the same time being evasive. Round three began with some wariness on part of both fighters, each trying to take advantage of the other's weaknesses. After some probing punches by each of them, Pug found an opening to deliver a damaging one-two combination of a left and right hook to the midsection. Again, the grimace on the face of Brawler indicated that a sensitive area had been revisited. Kowalski did not like the fact that he had been hurt twice by those body punches and was a bit angered because of the fact. He lost his cool and charged in for the attack only to be greeted by a well-placed left jab to the head. He backed off having to shake off the cobwebs that resulted from that powerful lefthand punch. This further infuriated him, and he quickly backed Freddie up against the ropes throwing several punches to his mid-section which were effectively blocked. Pug followed with a left jab and a blocked right uppercut to the jaw. This allowed him to get away from being backed up against the ropes. End of round number three.

B.J. praised him for following his advice and told him to be careful and to seek out an opportunity to end the fight. Round number four started with a considerable amount of evasive tactics. Freddie was patiently waiting for his opponent to bring the fight to him and was looking for that break to end the contest. At the same time, Kowalski was looking to send Freddie to dreamland. It was time to put Freddie away and his opponent threw caution to the wind and came charging in. Freddie held his ground and greeted him with a hard left jab. Another unappreciated action further infuriated Brawler, who was considered to be a well-disciplined boxer. Again, Kowalski was going to carry the fight to him and this time his action prompted the referee to cry out, "Stop boxing." That message was a result of a low blow. Pug was sent to his knees forcing him to stay down for a count of eight before he was able to rise. He was sent to a neutral corner in order to recover and continue on with the match. Enzo was at wits end because he was not able to be of help to his buddy. After about three minutes, Pug notified the referee that he was able to continue on with the bout. The ref called the fighters to the middle of the ring, warned Kowalski that another two fouls would disqualify him and make Pug the winner. He told them to touch gloves, return to their assigned corners and come out fighting. No sooner than they got back to exchanging blows, the bell sounded, ending the round. Pug received a considerable amount of remedial attention on his return to his corner. Two worried people were making sure he would be in good shape to fight the next round.

The two belligerents came out punching. The Brawler knew he had to win by knockout, because he figured Freddie to be ahead in points. Pug was on the receiving end of a right cross that he was able to fend off. He backpedaled a bit then suddenly stopped and stood his ground. Kowalski wanted to carry the fight and moved in on Freddie. He set out to greet Pug with a one-two combination that would end this bout. Freddie anticipated his move and did the unpredictable. He assumed a standard stance and warded off both the jab and the right cross. He then quickly switched to a southpaw stance and let loose of a powerful right jab to the face followed by a devastating left hook to Kowalski's midsection. The result of a beautifully executed one-two combo sent him down on his knees writhing in pain. He was unable to continue and was down for the ten count. Freddie followed what most boxers consider the number one rule in boxing, to be unpredictable.

The crowd, which was totally partisan and in favor of Kowalski before the bout had begun, were now cheering wildly for the new guy on the block. Freddie was showered with accolades of every description. His trainer and corner man were bursting with pride. Enzo blurted out that he was buying pizza, which brought a big grin to Freddie's swollen face. The victor was nonchalant about the whole rigmarole and ready to go get a pizza and celebrate that way. He did feel like he'd

had to battle hard and merited the treat. That fight was
to be the last as a Golden Glover. He wanted to go
professional so that he could earn money to help B.J.
solve his problems. It certainly was a fitting ending,
considering the hard work he had put in preparing to
enter the sport.

CHAPTER TWENTY-EIGHT:

IT'S TIME TO TURN PRO

B.J. had been busy for almost a month, making all of the necessary preparations for the move to the pro ranks. He was fortunate to get a match with a fighter who had been a promising contender for some time. He was badly beaten by a boxer who outclassed him. A match that never should have been arranged. Now he was trying to move back up in the ranks. Most of the people in the know in the boxing game did not give him much of a chance to make that happen. He would never reach that peak again. B.J. was of the opinion that the match would be good for Freddie's introduction into the pro ranks. He would be facing an opponent who had good name recognition and was viewed favorably in the boxing world. B.J. also liked the fact that Tiger Malone was not living up to his past reputation. He no longer was befitting of the moniker he was tagged with. There was no tiger left in his tank. It would be provident for his fighter not to be matched up with the old Tiger Malone. Freddie would be facing a fighter, who prior to his last three defeats, was an up-and-comer. In his professional career, he was credited with ten victories in thirteen outings before his saddened slide.

B.J. was unaware of the fact that Malone was reportedly coming out of his timidity stage and seemed to be headed towards becoming his old self again. There was joy once again in his camp as he was preparing for the upcoming event. Everything in Freddie's camp was going perfectly. Everyone was in a positive mood and training was proceeding as planned. The training phase continued on for the next three weeks in preparation for the big event.

There was a slight chill in the air on this early September evening in Chicago, Illinois. There was also a lot of excitement from a sizeable crowd of about two thousand avid fight fans. Many were there to see if Tiger Malone would show signs of coming back to his old form. There were also those who wanted to see what the young Golden Glover had to show in his first professional bout. The two dressing rooms were a buzz of activity. Enzo for the first time was engaged in wrapping his buddy's hands. It had to be perfect. He wanted to make sure those hands were well protected. B.J. was going over last-minute details with his charge advising him of every important detail about his opponent. The last bit of information delivered was concerning Malone's approach to the fight. His take on the matter was that Malone was still in his timid mode, and Pug would have to carry the fight to him. His final words were, "Keep your head in the game. Be prepared for any eventuality. Good luck, champ. This is your night to shine."

The two gladiators were summoned to proceed to the ring. It was fight time. The two preliminary matches were finished and did nothing to excite the anxious fans. Malone was greeted with an abundance of good luck wishes. He also heard several well-wishers offer their hopes for a comeback victory for him tonight. Freddie was well pleased with the manner in which he was received. Some in the crowd were advising him that they were here to see his first pro victory. Others were referring to him as champ, probably as a result of his Golden Glove victory. The air was electric. The crowd noise exhilarated the newcomer and tended to elevate his senses.

Once inside the ring they both pranced around, each exhibiting a bit of wariness about their opponent. The newcomer was having a bit of concern regarding his foe's ring experience. The veteran fighter felt a bit uneasy over facing the notorious up-and-comer. They were both feeling the weight of the occasion.

The referee told them to go to their corners. The ring announcer implored the crowd to rise and introduced the singer of the National Anthem. A gifted young lady then provided the hushed crowd with a most beautiful rendition of the song. The crowd stayed standing and applauded her effort for an extraordinary length of time. Freddie had a lump in his throat and tears were visible on his cheeks. It was an exciting and emotional experience for him. He was visibly shaken because of the immense pride he had for his wonderful country. It was time for him to gather himself and focus on the task set before him.

The ring announcer then announced the name of each fighter and called out the color of their trunks in order to identify each of them. Back in their corner, they awaited the call to engage. A few seconds later the referee barked out the call to come out fighting. They both came out to the center of the ring and Malone wasted no time engaging his opponent. The move on his part surprised everybody and Freddie recollected some of his trainer's last words. The last thing he expected was what had just taken place. Now his approach to the fight was certainly different from what he had anticipated. Malone was there to avenge his previous defeats and to get back on the come-back trail. Pug had a fight on his hands from an experienced professional. There were considerable exchanges dealt out during the first round without any real damage to either of the fighters. Freddie was on the receiving end of a good volley as the round began. He felt a little sting of the right to his head and welcomed the cold towels that were applied to his face.

Round two featured a rousing bit of action with both fighters on the offensive. The crowd was compelled to rise to their feet on several occasions when neither boxer would give ground. It was this toe-to-toe fighting that was not expected by the Ryan camp. Malone was in swarmer mode, exactly the type of fighter that was most unwelcomed by Freddie. He knew he was going to have to modify his tactics and soon. He did not want to become a punching bag for an aroused tiger.

Round three saw a different Pug Ryan in the ring. He was constantly on the move. He was not going to play into Tiger Malone's hands. He was bouncing in, taking a few shots, then retreating, careful not to be caught up against the ropes. This constant in and out pattern was wearing on Malone, and it was tiring him out while trying to plant a good right to Pug's head. Youth was on Freddie's side, and he was going to use it to his advantage. He kept up the in and out movement while being able to land one very good right cross that got Malone's attention.

It was much of the same for the next eight rounds, which found Pug to be the aggressor landing more solid blows than Malone. During the fight, the referee was constantly advising Pug to be mindful of his low punches. It was a constant stream of, "Get those punches up, Ryan." On several occasions his admonitions were met with a chorus of boos. The ref was the only one who was not aware that the punches he was calling out were well above the navel.

The final round found an exhausted Tiger being pursued by Pug. There was no let-up on Ryan's part. A minute into the round, Pug landed a solid left hook that found Malone unable to regain himself and left very vulnerable. Pug, for whatever reason backed off, knowing he was way ahead on points. He did not want to KO the veteran. The crowd was calling for him to finish him off, but Pug allowed Malone to get his feet under him again. Malone shook off the blow and returned to continue fighting. He moved around the ring, avoiding any contact with Pug. This action elicited a thunderous uproar from a disappointed fight crowd. Pug tried to move in on him to no avail and managed to land a few glancing punches on the retreating Malone. The round ended without any further damage being done. It was a very disappointing ending to a performance that the crowd had witnessed. What they did see and liked was a good showing by a young pro in his first outing. Everyone was bewildered by Pug's hesitancy to finish his opponent off.

It was decision time. The three judges huddled for an extended period of time while an anxious crowd waited for their decisions. Judge number one ruled the fight a draw while the second judge awarded the fight to Pug Ryan. It was his opinion that Pug had won seven of the twelve rounds. Judge number three shared the opinion of judge number one ruling for a draw. In a case such as this, a majority draw decision, the fight is recorded as a draw.

Upon revealing the decision of the three judges, the crowd showered him with their disapproval of their vote. Shouts of "robbers," "kill the ref," "terrible decisions," and various other slurs were let out to show discontentment they had for the ruling of the two judges.

Back in the locker room of Freddie Ryan, there was gloom hanging over the whole entourage. B.J. was in a reflective mood due to Freddie's reluctance to finish Malone off when he had the opportunity to put him away. Enzo was disappointed that his good friend was not treated fairly by the judges. He knew full well that Pug had won more rounds than with what he was credited. He felt the referees constant reference to low punches had cost him several rounds. Others in the room insisted that Freddie had carried the fight from the second round on. He was the aggressive fighter in every round and scored more effective punches than his opponent. That most of Malone's punches were either errant or of the powder puff variety was the feeling of the majority present. Freddie was remorseful that he did not pursue Malone to finish him off. He also regretted losing the opportunity to collect the bonus that was to be paid to the winning boxer. He felt it could have been a big help to B.J. for the purpose of settling some of his indebtedness. Everyone left with an empty feeling because of the results from the night's activities. A positive result coming from the match was the fact Freddie was able to present B.J. with a fourteen-thousand-dollar stipend, a fifty percent share of his contract payment.

CHAPTER TWENTY- NINE:

LIVING DOWN THE DEFEAT

Upon return to Paducah, Freddie and B.J. were engaged in a serious conversation in the privacy of his office. B.J. began by admonishing his fighter for not finishing off his opponent. "You disregarded my advice to you about not allowing an opponent to recoup and have the opportunity to come back and beat you. I told you that I would not be your manager if you were unwilling to give it your all. A fighter you give another chance could very well put you away the very next round. He is fighting to win. You do not grant him the opportunity to come back. What did it cost you? For one thing, a win. It also cost you a loss of a move up in ranking and no winner's bonus. It will also affect the amount you can expect to be paid in an upcoming bout. You had the match won if only you would have continued on the attack. Most of all, you have disappointed me. I trusted that you would fight to win and protect yourself in the process. I am not about to be a party to anything that I feel may contribute to your being hurt or crippled. Do I make myself clear?" "Yes sir, I'm sorry." "Now I need to know that when you put the gloves on again you are there to fight. As far as I am concerned there will be no next time unless you tell me you are hearing me, and that you can assure me you have the will to fight."

"You have my word. I have heard all you have said, and I can tell you I will be there to fight and to give all I have to come away with a win."

"On a different note, I did like most of your performance except for pulling off the fight as you did. There are a few things we will have to work on, so we will start on that today. I will be trying to arrange another match, and hopefully I have some success in doing so. Your unforgiveable snafu will make it harder to get a contract with a better fighter. His manager might feel you will cost him at the gate. The less attendance, the smaller the amount he is going to collect. Winning performances attract fight fans, halfhearted efforts do not."

Training proceeded according to plan and the warrior was being shored up by his diligent trainer. Finding a match was not proceeding as B.J. would have liked for it to go. The fighter, in the meantime, was working hard to please his trainer. He wanted to win for him, and he wanted to earn more money to relieve the pressure on a man he had come to respect and love. Enzo, who was ever present when he was not at work at the store, was there to help however he could. He would say, "All of the associates at the store are still buzzing about how you were wrongfully deprived of a win. They are all pulling for you and wish you the best in your next outing."

Two months passed since his last fight, and in all of the conversations Freddie had with his parents, there was no mention of the fact he was engaged in boxing. It was apparent to him that they had not become aware of the fact. If they were, they certainly did not let on they knew anything about it. He definitely had no intention of informing them about his participation in the sport. It was much to his liking that things were as they stood. He figured that if they knew of his present occupation, it would only give them something to worry about.

What he did find out in his many conversations was that all was well with them. His mom was very happy about the pleasant Charleston weather conditions. She was very involved and was enjoying the various organizations she was active in at church. His dad could not be happier with his new position and was heavily embroiled in the demands of his new job. He was ecstatic over the wide variety of bird species he was encountering on their frequent visits to Kiawah Island. It was a bird lovers paradise. The frequent gator that he encountered on several of his excursions dampened his desire to stray too far off the main roads. He assuredly made a wise decision regarding that matter. He missed them dearly. It was hard to accept being apart and that this would probably be the way it would remain for the rest of their lives.

Training was going as planned, but something was missing. He could not develop the killer instinct that boxing required of him. He would do everything required of him for one reason only. His desire to please and financially help his friend B.J. was a driving force. The problem resulted in him not enjoying his grudgingly accepted profession. There was no elation felt over any of his prior wins. There was no pride of achievement other than what came from the help he was able to offer B.J.

It seemed like an eternity had passed since his last bout and he was anxious to get on with business. A lucky break was presented to them due to the bad luck of another fighter. Cecil Bones was scheduled to fight against a boxer on the rise, seeking to get a shot at the reigning champion. In a sparring match he had been the victim of a low-blow and suffered from a trauma-induced ruptured appendix. One man's misfortune had become another's good fortune. Freddie was given the opportunity to replace Bones because the manager of Bosco, the contender, had no other choice. There was no other fighter available to choose from.

And so it was that the card of Jake the Snake Bosco and Freddie Pug Ryan was to replace the previously matched event. Freddie would not get the guaranteed purse amount that Bones would have earned. His fight history did not warrant the need for the large amount that was offered. B.J. was quite pleased with the bid and advised Freddie to accept the amount. There was no hesitation on his part and the contract was signed and sealed.

Ten days later, a refreshed Freddie Ryan was entering the ring after being tended to by Enzo. A raucous crowd of about eighty-five hundred fans were on hand to watch a match that now featured a replacement for the original challenger who was to face Bosco. The change in the card did not seem to dampen the enthusiasm of the fans in attendance. They were there to see the Snake earn a win and get a shot at fighting the existing champion.

Once more, his trainer looked Pug in the eye and said, "You know what you are here for, and you certainly know how to get it done. This is the chance of a lifetime for you, a chance to be recognized and move up in the ranking. This is your night to shine. Are you going to make it happen?" "I am here to fight and to win. I will give it my best shot." An excited and loyal buddy patted him on the back and asked, "Am I in for an answer to my prayers, a decisive victory by the best fighter in his weight class?" Freddie responded with, "God willing, it will be so."

Neither B.J. nor Enzo had much to cheer about in the first four rounds. Freddie might possibly have been awarded one of the four rounds. Bosco was aggressive and very active. He was constantly on the move and constantly leashing volleys. In the fifth round, Pug really gave his corner reason to worry as he slipped while moving in on Bosco. The seasoned boxer did not miss the opportunity to knock Freddie down for a count of eight. It was fortunate that only a few seconds remained in the round. It was not enough time for the Snake to seal the victory.

There was good bit of action in his corner. Advice, along with warnings were being handed out by B.J. while Enzo was doing all he could to refresh a battered Pug. They had to revive him in order for him to survive and have a shot at a victory.

The sixth round presented a different picture. There were now two aggressors in the ring. Freddie came out flitting around the ring like a moth hovering over a lighted bulb. He was fast and flashy. It was apparent that he had been rejuvenated, which was not to the liking of the Snake. Whatever it was that fostered this behavioral change was quite pleasing to the two fellas in his corner. Within the first ten seconds, Freddie had already landed two effective punches to the Snake's face. Blood trickled down his cheek from his nose. As the Snake attempted to wipe away the trickling blood, a combination left jab, and a right hook found it's mark in his midsection. They were crippling blows that sucked the air out of him. He was in trouble. His knees were buckling when once more, a right to his head sent him sprawling to the canvas. The fight was over. He could not get to his feet before the ten count was announced by the referee. Freddie Pug Ryan had redeemed himself, fighting the type of fight he was very capable of doing.

Freddie's hand was lifted high above his head by the ref who was now declaring him the winner of the fight. B.J. and Enzo were cheering loudly, blending in with the cheers of almost every fan present. The place was in an uproar. The crowd did not expect what they had just witnessed and showed their pleasure for the performance Pug had treated them with. It was a fast and furious finish executed by a well-trained and proficient fighter. They certainly had got their money's worth from a fighter on the rise.

CHAPTER THIRTY:

LET THE GOOD TIMES ROLL

There was no longer a problem securing future matches. Managers were clamoring for the opportunity to contract matches and negotiate with B.J. for higher purses than they originally offered. He always ended up being the winner in prize money negotiations. There would be no more measly paydays like the one in the Bosco fight. He fought that fight for fifty thousand dollars less than what Bones was offered. One saving grace was his winning the victors prize, enabling him to split seventy thousand dollars with B.J. His buddy Enzo earned ten thousand dollars for his share. It was three thousand more than what was the normal amount of money he was entitled to receive. Everybody was happy, and eagerly looking forward to the next match. They didn't have to wait long. A week later they were matched up for a bout with another Welterweight crown seeker.

On Tuesday morning a call came from his mother, who was anxious to get answers to some questions. Maureen wanted to know, "Do you remember Emma Grant?" Robbie replied that he did not. "Well, do you remember her son Robbie? You were in school with him in your

High School days." "I do, he and I had played baseball together during our sophomore year. Why, did something happen to him?" "No, I just wanted to make the connection. Emma recently moved here and is a member in one of my church groups. She questioned me as to whether the up-and-coming young fighter her husband had read about was my son. She said the name of the fighter in the article was Freddie Ryan. Now I am wondering if that is a fact. Is that you they are writing about? If it is, you made no mention about it to me or your father." "It is me. I did not want to burden you and dad knowing I was in the fight game. I had a conversation with dad sometime back informing him that I might get involved. He even knew the reason for me doing so. Anyhow, I don't want either of you to be concerned about my participation." "I don't know what to say. I am happy for you if you are. We will not be seeing any of the fights you may be scheduled for in the future. You do know we will be with you in spirit, right at your side cheering you on. My only hope is that you will not incur serious injury because of your decision." "I prepare hard in order to be able to avoid the possibility of that happening. I do not ever knowingly put myself at risk while engaging in a match. I have two good corner men who do everything possible they can to alert me if I were endangering myself. Now that you know what I am doing, promise me that you will avoid needless worry. I'm sorry to have to cut the conversation short, but I am late in leaving for a training session. Goodbye for now, love you. Make sure to pass the message on to dad."

Freddie had been engaged in nine matches in which he was declared the winner of every match. Two of the matches were declared as unanimous decisions by the judges. Two others were by way of technical knockouts after he had inflicted a great deal of damage to the two opposing fighters. The remaining five fights were the result of knockouts accounting for the victories. He was the winner of nine consecutive bouts. As a result of his tremendous successes, he was declared the leading contender for a match against the reigning Champion in the Welterweight division. All of the pomp and commotion did not change the person he was. He remained the same old Freddie Pug Ryan. He was the non-belligerent youth who donned boxing gloves for one reason only. It was for the purpose to help a friend, his trainer, out of a difficult financial problem. He had more than satisfied the need that found him now on the precipice of becoming a World Champion boxer. B.J. was no longer in debt and was now free of the constant prodding of the Internal Revenue Service (IRS) agent who was assigned to his case. He could breathe freely once more and the relief he felt was an aid in relieving the tension under which he was living. The near-thirty-year-old boxer had also become a medicine man, a healer, for his dear friend. He had only one goal. He was not seeking the title he would receive upon his winning the bout. What he wanted was a win for B.J. and Enzo.

What was becoming known as the fight of the century, was only a few weeks away. All of the preliminary dealings had been completed. Freddie's contract called for a three hundred-thousand-dollar payment for his participation in the match. A winner's take was set at one hundred-thousand dollars. Ticket sales were brisk, and an attendance estimate was set at fifty thousand paid ticket holders.

The next week and a half would find two intrepid combatants engaged in some rigorous training. The purpose being for one was to retain his title. While for the other it was to wrest the title away. The so-named fight of the century sparked the question: Could the reigning champ withstand the fury of a boxing phenomenon? The answer coming from most of the ardent boxing fans was that he would be unable to retain the crown. He was being identified as not having what it takes to stand up to the talent of the contender.

The impending battle elicited an enormous amount of speculative conversation. Fight fans everywhere were engaged in differences of opinion regarding the outcome. The Champion, Rusty Grossinger, had been a favorite for many years and maintained a large fan base of loyalists. Freddie Ryan, in the short span of time he was fighting as a pro, had attracted an exceptionally large number of fans who saw him as the favorite. The excitement building up to fight night was rising to a crescendo level. It was a madhouse the day before as well as the day of the momentous matchup.

The big night had arrived. The two combatants were in their locker rooms being attended to by their cornermen. While being carefully attended to, Rusty was instructed to make sure he avoided Ryan's right-handed punches. Freddie's hands were being taped and a wary Enzo was paying particular attention to his boxer's right hand. He had noticed swelling occurring during the last several sparring matches. He also noticed that Pug was not throwing a lot of right-handed punches. Enzo questioned him regarding his reluctance to use the right hand as he normally did and was told he was trying out a different punch sequence. Enzo did not think it was a truthful answer that accounted for the new behavior. As he finished wrapping the right hand, he noticed some grimacing taking place. A concerned Enzo questioned, "Is everything alright with you? Your hand seems to have swollen more since the last wrapping." "I am fine, there is no pain associated with the swelling. I think it's a result of an insect bite." Enzo was reluctant to mention it to B.J., feeling that Freddie would say if there was a problem. Freddie was going into the fight with what he knew could possibly hamper his performance. He did the same thing twice before and came out the winner. Pug was certain that all would be well, and that he would be able to fight as usual. He had to win for B.J. and Enzo.

CHAPTER THIRTY-ONE:

THE FIGHT OF THE CENTURY

It was time for the two to touch gloves and retreat back to their corners. The crowd noise was at its highest level of the star-studded evening. The mild temperature in the stadium suited everybody, especially the gifted boxers who were there to please the anxious crowd. The bout had not even started, and the fans were already on their feet waiting for the show to begin. The front rows were packed with all sorts of dignitaries. The mayor and his guests were privy to front row ringside seats and were as enthusiastic as the rest of the crowd. The last shout of the evening before the fight had begun was from Enzo, saying, "We're with you Freddie. Go get him. You will sure look good wearing the championship belt."

The ref called for the boxers to come out fighting, an invitation to which they quickly responded. Grossinger was the first to start throwing leather, which missed the intended target. Two rapid left-hand jabs landed on the side of Freddie's right shoulder. The punches had been deflected and had no effect on him. They were followed by a combination of a left jab and a right hook. The jab was a wake-up call to Pug's head and the vicious right hook was blocked by his right hand. Freddie countered with a solid left to Rusty's mid-section which got his attention. There was no right-hand punch to follow the damaging jab. Rusty backed off and was moving all about the ring in order to avoid further contact. He regained his composure just as round one came to an end.

Round two ended up being somewhat quieter than the first. They were both trying to feel each other out while evading each other. It appeared that neither one was eager to assume an aggressive approach. The crowd reaction was very different than that of the first round. They were not treated to the same tempo as in round number one. They were yearning for some excitement.

Round three provided exactly what they were seeking. Both fighters landed some very effective punches. B.J. and Enzo were becoming aware of the lack of right-hand punches from Pug. His right hand did come into play on several occasions. It was being used to effectively block some haymakers leveled at Freddie's head. While blocking one of Grossinger's punches there seemed to be a sign of discomfort on Freddie's part. While back-pedaling in order to avoid further contact, he pulled his hand into his side. It appeared he was seeking to soothe some of the pain he was experiencing. Round three ended with no further damage.

Round four was a whirlwind of action. Both fighters stood toe-to-toe while delivering violent blows to each other. The crowd was on their feet again, wildly cheering for their favorite boxer. It seemed that the punishment being handed out would not come to an end. It continued in that way until the bell brought an end to the frenzy.

In Freddie's corner, there was considerable concern about his condition. Some cut work was taking place to stop the bleeding to his right cheek. Cold towels were administered to help refresh a game combatant who showed no signs of giving in. B.J. wanted an answer. "Freddie, do you feel okay? Do you want to call it quits?" "Not at all. As long as I am standing, this fight will continue. What is bot..." Before he was able to finish the conversation, Freddie headed out to fight another round.

Round number five saw some different tactics being employed. Freddie was moving in and out while circling the ring. His intentions were to keep his distance, become a moving target, and wait for an opening to unleash a series of punches. He would patiently wait for an opportunity to revert to a southpaw stance. He employed this strategy once before. It was employed as a stealthy offensive move on that occasion. This time it would be necessary to employ it for defensive purposes. It was his means to survival. The round ended with a good bit of infighting, none of which was explosive or did harm to either of them.

Back in his corner he had the opportunity to finish the conversation that abruptly ended before being called out for round five. He queried of B.J., "What is it that is bothering you?" "Your wellbeing. I know your right hand is bothering you. I can see you are unable to use it as an offensive weapon, as well as for defensive purposes. I do not want you to risk your career. There will be other opportunities to vie for a chance at the Championship." "You are right. My intentions are to end it in the next round if the opportunity presents itself.

The crowd was clamoring for more action much like they had experienced in rounds one and four. They wanted to see a knockout end this bout. Round number six started out much like number five. Freddie searched for an opening while defending against Rusty's many attempts to nail him with a knockout punch. Freddie's defensive moves enabled him to stave off a good many of the punches thrown at him. He also was able to get in two very punishing left jabs that really stung his worthy opponent. The opportunity never availed itself for him to put an end to the fight. They would continue on to round number seven.

B.J. greeted him with, "Nice job. Your lefts hurt him a bit. Do you think you can put him away with your left?" "That is my intention. I am waiting for the right time to make it happen." They both faced each other off for the beginning of round number seven and went right to it. It was not long before Freddie got the opportunity he was looking for. He converted to a southpaw stance and fired two very solid punches to Grossinger's face that nearly knocked him off of his feet. He recovered from that action, and they exchanged several more punches, none of them doing any harm. The referee separated them, presenting another opening that Pug took advantage of. He let loose of a lightning-fast left-handed uppercut that floored Rusty. He was saved by the bell just as the ref had counted out number nine.

The crowd once again was energized from the action that had just taken place. The stadium was going wild. Nobody expected to see Grossinger on the canvas, let alone remaining down for that long of a count. He had barely been able to rise to his feet. He was stunned by the power behind the punch that nearly did him in.

A lot was going on in Grossinger's corner. They wanted to get him revived in order to be able to compete in round eight. The efficient work of his cornermen enabled him to answer the call to the eight round. There was still concern over in the other corner, but they were given reason for hope of another victory along with a coveted Championship title.

There would be no trickery allowed by the stunned boxer as he warily approached his young, reenergized opponent. Rusty entered this round with the full knowledge that he was facing an excellent boxer. However, he wasted no time going after Pug, knowing he was nearly incapacitated from the previous seven rounds. He was firing on all cylinders and Pug was warding off punch after punch. He was hardly able to respond back due to the fury of the attack. He had to back out and try to recoup. Pug did manage to break away and somewhat recover from the onslaught. Although he was not totally recovered, he went on the attack. While engaging in some heavy exchanges, he managed to land another left that once again sent Rusty down on the canvas. Rusty stayed down for a long count and got up wondering what his fate might be if he were facing a healthy Pug who had use of his right hand. He had to finish Pug off. Rusty went to work throwing as much leather as his exhausted body would allow him to do. A hard right, which was blocked by Pug's right hand, almost brought him to his knees. The pain from the punch was unbearable. His hand was on fire. Rusty took advantage of his predicament and started to unmercifully pound him in the face. Enzo, his cornerman, and dear friend, could not bear to witness what was unfolding. He quickly grabbed the towel and flung it into the ring. The fighting was ended. Enzo's merciful act ended in a TKO victory for still Champion Rusty Grossinger. There was an eerie silence, unreminiscent of what is expected from a large crowd of fight fans. It seemed that the outcome was not what majority of the fans had hoped for.

A game and haggard Freddie Pug Ryan sat with his two friends and flashed a broad smile aimed at B.J. and Enzo. His friend was in the process of removing the gloves and tape from his hands, when Freddie said, "You are doing this for the last time for me. I have accomplished what I set out to do. My boxing days are over. I am sorry that I could not have earned a Championship title for both B.J. and you. I gave it all I had to give. I have no desire to ever fight again."

CHAPTER THIRTY-TWO:

PERSEVERANCE PAYS OFF

Freddie Ryan never did go back to Swanson's Supermarket to work there again. It was a different life that he engaged in after his fighting days had ended. His will to enter pro boxing, something he really did not aspire to do was motivated by an unselfish reason. The result of his participation in the sport brought him many rewards for which he was very grateful. Not winning the championship did not cause him any regrets whatsoever. What did offer him much pleasure and satisfaction was what he was able to accomplish for B.J. The amount of money he was able to split with him from his boxing earnings saved B.J. from bankruptcy and further problems with the IRS. His lifetime buddy, Enzo, was also handsomely rewarded for his participation as a cornerman and cut man. What he cherished most, and was happy about, was his ability to perform these generous acts for his friends.

Shortly after Pug's decision to end his boxing career, B.J. succumbed to the illness that he had been receiving treatment for. It was a sad day on which he was laid to rest. He was interred in a beautiful mausoleum that Pug and Enzo had designed for that purpose. It was patterned to resemble the best gym in Paducah. It seemed as if the whole town was at the cemetery after the celebration of his life at his church. The honor guard detail present at the burial site presented the folded flag to Freddie due to B.J. not having any surviving relatives. The receipt of the flag followed by the playing of taps brought about an overwhelming sense of grief to him. Many of the attendees were seen wiping away tears at the loss of a good man and devoted friend.

Pug and Enzo were willed the home that B.J. resided in, along with his remaining cash. Freddie relinquished his claim to the home and passed on his ownership to Enzo. It was where Enzo and his wife lived and raised a family of four wonderful children. The business was to become the property of the lad that did so much to brighten B.J.'s life. Pug, being in B.J.'s employ as the gym manager, made the change to owner a very smooth transition. Enzo, who retired from Swanson's replaced the outgoing manager. The two peas in a pod were now happily working side by side. Several years passed and a major change was in the process of being completed.

One early June morning, a crowd gathered to witness the grand opening of the new Number One Gym in Paducah, Kentucky. Pug and Enzo, the newly appointed partner in the business, were proudly showcasing their dream. The crowd in attendance was greatly impressed to what was a monument to the beloved previous owner. It was a much larger structure that stood beside the old gym. The structure, although built of sandstone, was purposely designed to resemble the old structure. The façade featured fine masonry work using blue Basalt stone. It was a work of art that was a welcome addition to the community. Above the door hung a beautiful newly designed sign reading, B.J.'s Gym. The interior was ultra-modern and featured brand-new equipment. There was not a body-building device available that was not contained in the magnificent edifice.

The old gym was to assume the identity of The Paducah Boys Club. It was befitting that Mr. Fred Gaines, who had recently retired from Swanson's Supermarket, would become the Manager of the club. It was more of a charitable position since the stipend he would receive would not support a single person. Bruno Balicki was to assume the position of caretaker which required considerably more hours and much more responsibility. His position merited a handsome salary paid for from whatever charitable monies were garnered. If there was a shortfall, the new owners of the gym would guarantee the funds required to meet the payroll. The club stayed in existence for eighteen years until the unexpected passing of Bruno, who died of complications from an earlier brain injury. It was believed to be an injury that he was dealt by his father in his early youth. Freddie and Enzo eventually donated the building to a charitable group that converted it into living quarters for the homeless.

Freddie married Mary Lee Bancroft, a neighboring lass, who was a guest at his eighteenth birthday celebration.

They lived in the home that was left to her upon the passing of her surviving father. Mary Lee and Pug, who raised three boys, were heavily involved in community activities. Eventually, Mary Lee became the president of the Chamber of Commerce. She held that position until failing health required her to slow down the pace. During her tenure, Pug became the Parks and Facilities Director. His sterling performance in that position caught the notice of an appreciative citizenry. He earned the respect and votes of a majority of the townspeople who helped sweep him into the office of City Mayor. It was a position he would hold for a period of twenty-two exciting years. He was recognized as being a forward-looking individual who led the way towards developing a welcoming and accommodating Park system for Paducah, the Jewel of Western Kentucky.

It was no accident that one of Enzo's sons became good friends with the oldest of Freddie's sons. Their friendship was forged much in the pattern of their fathers. It had been a long enduring one, cherished by each of them. Brad Enzo became an Admiral in the Coast Guard. A great deal of his life was spent on the river, which led to his choice of service. He was the fourth Admiral native to Paducah. The other three, Burch, Clifton, and Paro saw service during World War II. Dean Ryan, Brad's buddy, was nominated for the office of Mayor but did not accept the nomination. His ambition was to become an Air Force pilot. He accomplished his goal and presently serves as a Colonel at Laughlin Air Force Base. It is highly likely that he will represent Paducah as the lone General to serve his country. The only other was a General named Lloyd Tilghman who served on the Confederate side during the Civil War. Dean Ryan's impending promotion is months away from becoming a reality.

The other children from both families had represented themselves well with their lofty achievements and their many contributions to society. Their parents most assuredly played a great role in fostering those consequences.

Looking in on them today we find Enzo still handling the business functions at the gym. As the former boxing coach at the gym, he was responsible for turning out two Golden Glove Champions. He did have one young man enter into the pro ranks. It might be said that his trainee never did come close to achieving what one Freddie Ryan was able to do. The new boxing coach, and a very talented one, is Enzo's youngest son.

As for Freddie Ryan, he lives alone in a home next to his middle son, an attorney, who looks in on him daily. Freddie suffered a stroke shortly after the death of his loving wife, Mary Lee. He is quite capable of fending for himself for most of his daily needs but does require some helping hands at times.

It is not surprising that these two men were so revered and honored by everybody they had come in contact with. Their contributions to their city and country, along with that of their offsprings will long be remembered and saluted by all. The world is a better place due to the actions of these two, and others who followed and had chosen to emulate them. It is safe to say that the time spent at B.J.'s gym assuredly had transformed two young boys into men of great stature.

THE END

ABOUT THE AUTHOR

John Stanczak is a late blooming author who hails from the American heartland. Born in 1930 and raised in North Chicago, Illinois, an ethnic melting pot about an hour north of Chicago, John has lived a full and interesting life, providing plenty of fodder for his storytelling.

John served in the Army during the Korean conflict. While John never saw combat, he was badly injured while playing on his post's baseball team and spent months in the hospital and rehabbing. After leaving the Army, John married and raised four children in Waukegan, Illinois, the birthplace of the famous author, Ray Bradbury, who used Waukegan – called Green Town, Illinois in his writings – as the setting for several of his short stories.

John, together with his younger brother Jim, co-owned a bowling alley in Waukegan in the '70's, and then moved south of the Mason-Dixon line, where he owned and operated several fast-food restaurants, a golf supply store, a children's play center, and a custom blinds business.

Having finally worked all of that entrepreneurial spirit out of his system, John retired at the age of 81 to Brentwood, Tennessee, just outside of Nashville, where

the writing bug bit him . . . and he's been writing ever
since. While John has not yet reached the heights – or
the output – of Ray Bradbury, he has authored four
books since turning 90 and is currently working on his
fifth.

John's first book published in 2021 was truly a labor of
love: The Story of the Stanczak Brothers Baseball
Team: Baseball's All Brothers World Champions. The
book, originally to be co-written with his brother Jim
who died shortly before the writing began, told the
story of the most successful all-brothers baseball team
in American history; a team comprised of John's father
and nine of his uncles.

He followed that in 2022 with the publication of
Musings... An Old Man's Recollections of Life's Events,
a semi-autobiographical story about coming of age in
the late 1940's and early 1950's. Not content to write
just about the past, John branched out into children's
books with the 2023 publication of the illustrated book,
The Adventures of Buzzy the Bee & His Friends, which
was illustrated by one of John's daughters. John tried
his hand at pure fiction that same year, publishing
America, of Thee I Sing, a novel of historical fiction set
in rural Mississippi during the Great Depression.

John's writings are infused with his love of country, his
commitment to inspire his readers, and his desire to
raise the standard of discourse in our society.

To try to keep up with John, feel free to visit his
website: www.johnrstanczak.com.